CREATURE OF SIN

CREATURE OF SIN

ALFRED B. GLASER

CUTTING EDGE

ISBN-13: 978-1-970848-01-4

Published by
Cutting Edge Books
PO Box 8212
Calabasas, CA 91372
www.cuttingedgebooks.com

CHAPTER ONE

A SLENDER BROWN LEG, SOFTLY CURVED, the pink of the flesh showing through the satin skin, supple and smooth-muscled, with small knee and tapering slender foot, stretched on the leaf-strewn sand in front of me. I decided not to step on it, or over it. I could spill some of the beer from the bottle on it. The beer was still cold—would it sizzle? I wondered if the body on the thigh end of that leg was as nice as the leg. I also wondered if the rest of that body hidden under the low hanging willow bushes, like Eve, held a nice big red apple, a red apple with a chunk bitten out of it, waiting for me, not Adam, to take another bite—and get my brains smeared on the willow bushes.

I tore my eyes from the delectable leg and let them search the crowded beach, the sweep of the Ohio River, with the late afternoon sun blazing it into a path of splendor. The boulevard on the Cincinnati side buzzed and hummed with Sunday cars. Large and small pleasure boats on the broad river skurled, rolled and skittered. Motors humming, growling, and snarling.

Tacoma Public Beach is a huge river-made sandbar, sticking four hundred feet out into the vast slow bend of the Ohio River. From where I was standing, with the shapely brown leg stretched indolently in front of me, willow bushes grew thickly to where the sand met the soil. Their wispy branches, covered with slim pointed leafage, reached down and mixed with the dirty sand.

The willow bushes add vastly to the popularity of the beach. By day they are the dressing-rooms for all. For the more venturesome, or bold, or those who don't care, they stand silent watch over the straining bodies, the husky voices, the giggling yield. At night, after the sun sinks into the flaming Ohio River in the west, they become suffused with humming insects, small bright fires, with dancing flames, the clink of bottles, soft sighs, raucous laughter, fluttering moans, the slap of bare hand on bare body, a vicious curse on the mosquito. Song, sigh, and quickly drawn breath. A jungle of sex.

The brown leg twitched slightly, muscles shivering delightfully. My eyes traveled its full length, spotted a small ant digging industriously on the inside, tender part of the thigh. So much of the leg was exposed, with part of the smooth hip-joint peeping out from under the willows, that it would be almost impossible for the rest of the body to have on a bathing suit. My pulse quickened at the thought, throbbed lightly in my head. Suddenly I envied the red ant on the smooth tender thigh.

"Brush it off!" The command was soft, amused.

"Huh?"

"Brush that ant off my leg, Lover-boy." The voice was definitely amused.

I went down on one bare knee, cupped my hand around the soft tender part of the leg, the flesh hot under my fingers, rubbed gently up as far I could go and back down. The leg squirmed a little. I rubbed again.

"Oh, damn," the amused voice said. "I know I could have gotten rid of the ant, but I'm not so sure about your hand. I guess it's all my fault for inviting you out here."

"The person who wrote the note?" I asked absently, squeezing the thigh.

"That must be Roscoe Todd's hand on my leg," she said throatily, like a voice with too much alcohol under the tongue. "Feels like a nice hand," she added, a laugh in her throaty voice.

"Nice leg," I said softly. "Where do I go from here?" I wanted to keep my mind and hand on that lovely leg, but the memory of the short note was crowding the sight of the lovely leg. I let my mind write the note on the satin skin. I had to keep moving my hand out of the way of my mind-writing. Best kind of writing I've ever done.

"I know all about the gambling," the note was re-writing itself on nice warm satin skin. "Come to Tacoma Beach Sunday at 7:30, wear blue bathing trunks, carry an open bottle of beer in your hand, but don't drink from it, and walk back and forth at the edge of the willow bushes. Come alone." No signature.

Now this brown leg and throaty voice. The hot thigh under my tingling fingers. The muscles in the hot thigh under my fingers bunched, the brown leg dug its heel into the sand and shoved itself back under the willow bushes.

"Hey!" I said. "Was that nice? As soon as my cold hand gets warm, you pull the stove away."

"The stove moved to a new location," the throaty voice taunted. "But if you want to re-warm your hand, scoot under, but make it quick." An edge of worry had crept into the voice.

I scooted under on two knees and one hand, the bottle of beer held in front of me, reminding myself that this girl might not be alone, that death could be crouched to spring from around her. Death from muscle-bound toughs well-practised in killing holds and assorted mayhem.

It wasn't bad, once you broke through the tangle of whip thin branches. Cool and sandy, the hot sun bouncing off the leafage. The girl was a dim shape, drawn back further into the willows, my eyes not accustomed to the shade. I could see old beer bottles, cigaret butts, paper bags—and those things that people leave lying around that dislike the idea of parenthood. I could see no one except the owner of the throaty voice. But you couldn't see far in among those willow bushes. I looked searchingly at the dim shape of the girl, while my sight adjusted to the shadows.

The girl was covered with nothing but a few pieces of gaudy cloth. Not a few pieces—just two. The halter fit the swelling breasts too soon. Much too soon, leaving soft bulges above and below. The triangle piece of cloth was knotted at each hip. Where it passed between the thighs it wasn't an inch wide. And here, too, the flesh bulged and pushed, trying to get out from under the confining fabric. I lifted my eyes slowly to her face.

The way she was sitting, leaning slightly forward, her hands buried in the sand, threw her features in sharp relief. The chin was a little too wide. The angle of the jaw swept up too fast to the small ears, but the cheekbones were wide, the eyes big and grey, with sooty lashes and thin eyebrows. The lips were passable, which means they were kissable. The nose was a little too broad at the base and not pointed enough. The hair that swept back from the low forehead was long and bleached, curling softly where it brushed her shoulders.

"Had a good enough look?" she asked, sinking backwards until the trunk of a willow bush supported her head, her fulsome body resting in the sand, her feet, with the legs slightly spread, touched my knees. "Pull yourself up close and talk quiet. You can drink your beer if you want to." She patted the sand alongside her hip.

I ignored the invitation. The view was better from here. I squatted back on my haunches, ducking my head to keep it out of the bushes. I offered her the beer silently, then poured some down my throat when she shook her head. I wiped my mouth with the back of my hand.

"Mrs.——?"

"Miss Thomson—Sheila. Make it Sheila."

"Okay, Miss—Sheila. Like you asked in the note, I'm definitely interested in gambling. More interested in who's running it. I don't know why you want to give me information. Unless you want to make some money, one way or the other." I watched her face closely, saw not a flicker of interest. "You probably know that I'm a counselor, not a lawyer. I'm not an investigator or private eye. I need a permit for that. So I counsel, which means that people who get into trouble gambling come to me with their troubles, usually because they lost more than they could afford, or the money didn't belong to them in the first place. But mostly because they found out afterwards that they had been played with a stacked deck and weren't big enough to fight the crowd that stacked the deck. For a percentage, I get that money back."

"Which is about as healthy as getting into bed with the girlfriend's roommate while she's filing her nails in the bathroom," Sheila said quietly.

"I've been shooting my mouth off in all the bars in Newport and no one has rammed a fist into it yet," I said quietly.

"I've heard that someone tried to," she said pointedly.

"Three someones," I answered. "They owed a widow fifteen hundred dollars. But they didn't think so. I don't know if I convinced them or not, but I got the fifteen hundred."

"Is that all you got?" she asked skeptically.

"No. I also got a night in jail. When I got out this morning, I found your note in my office. How much do you want to spill what you know?"

"I want a few questions answered first," she said huskily, wriggling her bottom to a more comfortable position, which action caused heat lightning to play around my belly.

"If you're in trouble, I'll help any way that I can," I said through suddenly dry lips, her nearness and near nakedness causing my breath to catch. I set the beer unsteadily in the sand, wrapped both hands around the bottle.

She looked into my eyes steadily for a full minute. Her tongue inched out and crawled slowly over her lips, moistening them to a dull shine. I watched the worry and fear mount into her grey eyes, and then something like panic.

"You got into a fight with those three characters last night— those three gamblers," she began in a rush. "I was told that you handled them like paper dolls—that you laughed in their faces while they tried to beat the hell out of you." She paused uncertainly.

"If I have occasion to get my hands on them again, I'll not only handle them like paper dolls—I'll rip them up like paper dolls in a child's vengeful hands. I'd kill them the same way I'd mash a rat, if I thought they were the right ones, the ones I'm looking for," I said viciously.

"What Big John said was true—" she said jerkily, in a throaty whisper, "—he said that … that you scared the fight right out of him, scared him so he couldn't move." She laughed, a caressing, husky laugh, with something intimate in it. That something caused my blood to burn, set a pulse to ticking in my throat.

She leaned forward, took me by the big muscle at the shoulder, and pulled me beside her. Her hand burned my skin felt cold against her fingers.

"That isn't what he said exactly," I spoke jerkily, fighting the emotion that her nearness brought. "He said that I scared the hell out of him, and he said it because he was still babbling like an idiot when the police got there."

"But Big John—" she said in a hushed whisper, looking at me, her warm body pressing into my shoulder, her bare hip resting against my bare leg. "I've seen him handle a man in each hand, toss them around like dolls. They said you broke his arm!"

In one quick motion I came to my knees, eyes searching the underbrush. I knew that I was in one helluva spot if this was a trap. It would be almost next to impossible to move in all this underbrush. Every sense alert, I listened. The muted sound of the crowd on the beach, the hum of insects. The very stillness breathed danger. I brought my eyes back to the startled Sheila.

"You had better talk—and fast!" I snarled. "You know those men who jumped me last night. You must know Big John—to know that his arm was broken!"

I grabbed her by the arms, lifted her face within inches of mine, conscious that her Bikini was slipping as her body was forced forward into a half-kneeling position.

"If this is a trap, with you as bait—I'll smash the bait into a bloody pulp the second the trap is sprung!" I breathed the words into her startled face, feeling the chill in them sharp against my teeth.

CHAPTER TWO

"IT'S NO TRAP—PLEASE!" she gasped. "I know Big John, Tim, and Jackson—I know the whole lousy bunch of them. Why do you think I'm asking you for help? Why do you think I want to get away from them—to get out of the whole rotten, stinking mess?"

"I'm sorry," I said, relaxing my grip on her arms. "You really haven't told me yet just why you're offering your help."

"I want out," she said helplessly. "I'm fed up with the damned gang, the muscle-bound morons, and the continual spying and sneaking. I want to be an entertainer, an actress—not a two bit whore!" she snapped the last on a note of utter futility; her body went limp under my hands, her eyes misted.

"You probably think that's what I am, anyway, meeting you like this, practically naked, using my sex on you. I can't blame you." She was half-sobbing, keeping herself under control with an effort. "I don't know you. I've never seen you before. Do you think that I'm that repulsive that I couldn't get a man? Do you think I would be here if this was a trap? They would have been waiting—not me!" She was breathing hard, her breasts straining at the slipping halter. She slipped both hands up my chest, onto my shoulders. Dug her fingers into the ropy muscles, the nails pricking my skin.

"I'm in trouble," she said pleadingly. "Bad trouble. I'm a small-time singer and dancer. I put on shows around here. Cincinnati, Newport, wherever I can make a tenspot. I know all the characters. It's part of my job."

She took a deep breath, leaned back from me in the darkening evening. One breast had escaped the halter, was standing up and glowing in its new-found freedom.

"I don't make much money. I won't pick up bed money." She looked at me defiantly. "I wouldn't be in this trouble if I did. They want me to. They laughed at me, said that they had time, said that fifty-sixty dollars a week would get to look awful small after a while." She ran one hand lightly through my curly hair, took one of the curls between her fingers, absently, straightened it out with an angry tug.

"It did," she said flatly.

She sat still, brooding, her hands back on my shoulders. I let the silence build. The sun was down in the west, it was almost dark here under the willow bushes. Sheila was half-reclining, her hands resting lightly on my chest, her almost naked body gleaming silkily in the gloom.

She shook herself suddenly, causing every bit of her flesh to quiver.

"Big John started it," she began abruptly. "He said that he felt sorry for me. Me being a good kid and all that. Not that I haven't had my fun." Her eyes flashed. "I'm not a girl that doesn't enjoy nature. A few days in the mountains, a night in a room. But with a partner I pick. Someone I like." Her voice was shivery, throaty again. Then it went hard, lifeless.

"So I fell for it. Like any kid from the sticks. Big John gave me a tip here, a tip there. I'd pick up twenty on this horse, fifty on that one. Everything was fine. New clothes, a better room. Even a used car for myself. Then the big thing. Big John believes in big things. He's big, so everything he does has to be big. He asked it as a favor....

"It was around two o'clock. I'd just finished a dance routine at the Frontier Bar. Big John came into my dressing room. He wanted to know if I would sit in on a card game, said that the tip came from Beverly Hills—you know, that big gambling palace just out of town—that a man and a doll had taken them for a roll. Big John said that his man out there had talked them into coming into Newport for a bust out dawn-to-dusk-to-dawn game. Beverly Hills locks up at three in the morning, and this guy and doll were hot." Sheila paused. She grinned wryly.

"So I went," she said grimly. "Big John to furnish the stake. I'm to get twenty percent of the take. I was to back his play. Do the wild playing on bad hands, so he could drift with the pot, pick it up with his good one. The old come-on-sucker-he's-bluffing game."

She leaned close to me, her bare breast where the halter had slipped brushing my chest, her warm mint-flavored breath on my face. Campfires had started to blink on the beach. The babble of voices had died down. A mosquito drew a quart of blood from my leg.

"That's about it," she said huskily. "We lost. We got took. Five grand took. After the guy and doll left, Big John sat scowling at me.

" 'Sheila, Baby,' he said, "can you dig up your thousand?'

"I laughed, but I was scared. A thousand dollars? 'Where do you think I can get a thousand dollars? And why should I?' I asked him. I was to get a share of the winnings. I wasn't supposed to pay a share of his loss. When I told him that it even sounded silly to me, Big John got up and walked around the littered table. He took me by the shoulders and lifted me to my feet.

" 'Then you'll earn it on your back!' he rasped. 'The boss is getting damned tired of your shaking it around these joints, getting guys to ask for it and the boss telling them it can't be had. I've kept you in money on small bets, but I can't dish out no grand for you. Besides, I'll see that you get the big games, the plush hotel parties. Those guys really toss money to a good mattress. The boss fronts for us, fixes for us, but we pay any money losses. We ain't supposed to lose on no damn fix, but we did. You have that money by tonight, or start bouncing the springs!' he finished coldly and left, leering at me as he went out the door.

"That was two days ago. I've been dodging him since. I heard some men talking about you and the fight. I called a girl I know to find out if it was true. She told me that Big John had a broken arm. You know the rest."

Her hands were pulling and twisting at my shoulder muscles, her mint flavored breath hot on my face.

"I'll do anything," she said frantically. "Anything but that. I'll spill my guts to you; tell you everything I know and suspect. Don't let those gorillas get their filthy paws on me." She was whimpering. She locked both arms around my neck, buried her face under my chin, her lips hot on my throat.

Blood was pounding in my head, the pit of my stomach felt like an elephant was standing on it and I knew if I tried to get to my feet, my legs wouldn't lift me.

I tried to force sanity into my flaming brain, even while my hands slipped around her bare belly, caressed the soft flesh.

Talk! Damn you—talk! I told myself numbly. Say something, anything, to break this spell, to curb the hot driving desire. I was after information, after those who got Kirk—those who got Kirk!

"The police are hell on that sort of thing in Newport," I said hoarsely. "Gambling, mayhem, murder, the cops ignore it, or seem to. But let one girl try to peddle and wham, she's out of town. You know that." A degree of sanity was coming back. The breast on my chest wasn't so hot, the pressure on my guts eased a little.

"You don't understand," she said in a throaty whisper, her lips wandering, hot on my throat. "I won't sell it. I have to stay in a room, next to a card game." She moaned softly in distress. "Without clothes. When a man wants to change his luck, or take a rest from the game, he comes in and—" She pressed herself to me, quivering. "Or when the game's over, they want a little dancing, a little lewdness on the card table—" I felt a hot tear drop on my chest, go burning its way down my belly.

I felt sick, sick with what she told me, sick with the flaming pictures her words created on my brain, sick with the desire that was tearing me apart.

"Don't worry," I said, my voice throbbing and distant in my own ears. "Don't ever worry about them again...."

She pulled her head back, a long mint-flavored sigh escaping her lips, quivering through her body. I dimly remembered not to crush my lips on hers, let my face slide down her cheek, the column of her throat. I fastened my teeth lightly into her neck at the shoulder. We strained together, on our knees. The halter came loose in my hands. Sheila arched her back, her breasts straining against me. She swayed with a gasp, went backwards into the sand.

The crash came from back in the willows, followed by a harsh curse at the log that broke under his weight. For a dull moment I clung to Sheila, my brain unwilling to release me from the emotion that held us welded together, her flesh burning and our breath torching in our throats. In the deep shadow I saw the willow bushes part, the blur of a face breaking through, followed by huge shoulders covered with a white and black checkered sportscoat.

CHAPTER THREE

THE BLOW THAT CAUGHT ME ON THE SIDE OF THE HEAD took my strength from me. I slumped, felt Sheila wriggling and squirming, felt myself rolled completely over. Through my fading senses I heard a shrill scream, trailing off into a strangled gurgle, then a grinding crunch that echoed in my ears, floating away to nothingness on pinwheeling sparks.

Those pinwheeling sparks got very small before they started getting larger and larger until they filled the whole of my world. I tried blinking my eyes. The sparks went away. I opened my eyes. A flashlight. My neck was twisted to a muscle straining angle, my head was roaring. I felt a finger across my mouth. I opened my mouth, felt the finger drive in. I bit down and ground my teeth together. The pressure left my neck muscles. A voice cursed hoarsely in my ear, hot alcoholic breath fanning my face.

Someone was on my back, arms wrapped around my head, twisting, intent on breaking my neck. Another man held a flashlight, kneeling in the sand, holding the beam on my face, his face a blur behind the light.

It hit me with a knot-tying spasm in the pit of my stomach, an unreasoning blazing rage flashing across my brain; I had about thirty seconds left to live.

I don't mind dying. I expect to die someday. But not this way, choking on dirty sand, my neck twisted and broken, flopping around like an axed chicken. And there was Kirk—did he die like this?

The sheer horror of the thought set me to humping and bucking, my hands spewing sand and twigs, until I got one leg under me. I came up, crashing through the willow bushes, the man riding my back bawling curses.

"Hey, leave him go!" The voice had panic in it. "Let's get the hell outta here. The girl screaming got those bums on the river heading this way. C'mon!"

The weight left my back, a driving blow from his foot sent me stumbling. I could hear the two of them scrambling in the willows. When they hit on one of the numerous paths, their sound vanished. Voices were shouting on the beach, coming nearer.

I got on my hands and knees, started crawling, feeling in the dark for Sheila.

"Sheila!" I called huskily. "Sheila!"

One groping hand came on a knee. I ran both hands up her body. It was warm, but still. Too still. My hands were on her face and I lifted her head. It turned easily, sloppily.

That grinding crunch I heard—her scream cut off so abruptly. I didn't feel for her heartbeat; Sheila was dead, dead with a broken neck.

The shouting and babble from the beach crowd was close. I could wait, and talk to the police, and go to jail. That would help no one. I could do nothing in jail. And I had something to do. I had some men to find, some murdering, brutal men that smashed with the power of their muscles. Now it was my turn. Only this time I knew someone to smash.

I slipped among the willows, not having time to find my bathing trunks. I found a path, followed the path to a rutted road. The low-slung outline of my Thunderbird Sporter was a welcome sight. I eased behind the wheel, twisted the key, flicked on the headlights and got out of there.

I put on my shirt while waiting for the stoplights in Dayton. I waited until I could pull under the bridge in Newport before I stopped and put on my pants and shoes. Feeling the lump on my head, I headed for my apartment.

I wanted a shower, a change of clothes. Things were going to start busting loose all over. I hoped savagely that Big John would be stubborn. That it would take a lot of busting before his jaw became unhinged.

CHAPTER FOUR

MY APARTMENT ON SARATOGA STREET IS A WALK-UP. Mike Doolan has the building, with a saloon on the first floor. He tried to be nice when I came from the Rental Agency and asked for my key. I didn't like his scarred face, nor his small, grey pig eyes—or the Cadillac parked in the slot in back. But we get along fine, though he doesn't like my doll face.

I went into the hall in the rear of the saloon and up the steps to my apartment. The two-story brick building was put up by the original settlers in the town. The Germans believe in double brick walls, large high rooms, big four-paned windows, with massive sills, hardwood floors. In spite of its hundred-year age, except for the style, the apartment might have been built yesterday.

The door from the outside hall opened into a smaller inside hall, with the kitchen, bathroom, bedroom—in that order—opening off the hallway on the left. The hallway itself opened into a spacious living room fronting on Saratoga Street. Two windows, draped with gold brocade, with green pull-down window shades, afforded an excellent view of the street and the reason why the apartment cost me only sixty a month furnished.

I went to the third door on the left and into my bedroom, stripped and carried my soiled and sandy clothing into the bathroom. I turned the shower on with a blast of water and stepped into the tub, pulled the shower curtain. The jetted water beat and stabbed my body. After the shower I picked up the bottle of nutrient oil and went back into the bedroom.

I finished with the nutrient oil. Checked to see if I needed a shave, found I didn't. I glanced at the clock on the dresser. Three minutes of nine. In the space of an hour and a half, I had held a beautiful girl in my arms, witnessed her murder and had come to within a split second of dying myself, with a broken neck. The muscles in my shoulders were getting a bit stiff and sore, the bump on my head had started to subside, but was tender to the touch.

I reached over and snapped the bedside radio on. The nine o'clock news from WCPO should be coming on the air. If any station had news on the murder at Tacoma, WCPO would have it. They did.

"... flash was just phoned in." The announcer was speaking in that mechanical excited voice so many use. "The victim of the sex maniac has been tentatively identified as Sheila Thomson, widely known local singer and dancer. It is apparent that she put up a terrific struggle after the maniac had dragged her back into the willow bushes. The police are still combing the area for clues and at this moment the only clue—and it is a valuable one—is the blue pair of swimming trunks. It is thought that they belong to the killer. The police refuse to comment on how long it will take them to trace the ownership of the blue trunks.

"Stay tuned to this station for further developments. In the meantime avoid the public beaches and lonely streets. If you have to go out, make sure that someone accompanies you."

I shut the radio off.

Bad. Very bad. But I expected it. I knew they would find those bathing trunks. As far as tracing them back to me, that was unlikely. The open air Bazaar had had a whole counter of bathing trunks. My purchase was one of many. The disinterested clerk probably wouldn't even be able to remember if her father had bought a pair. They might help in convicting after the owner was caught, but they would be no help in the catching.

I started dressing, selected a brown summer suit, with the new weave and tiny gold flecks, my mind on the murder.

Dayton was a small town. The few police and detectives the city boasted had many routine duties. They would give the murder as much time as they could, but unless they were able to "borrow" some talent from the tri-city area, they would have to drop the case. From what I had learned about the tri-city area, I doubted if they could borrow anyone. Not unless they could tie the murder up with something that happened in one of those cities. With what evidence they had, it would be next to impossible, unless a witness fingered me.

I let that roll around in my mind while I finished dressing. It was a possibility. If the gambling boss thought I was dangerous enough, he or she could have it done. Checkered sportscoat or the other thug could easily do it.

I didn't think that the gambling boss wanted any part of the police. He or she thought they had ways of their own. What would happen when and if those ways failed to work? No use borrowing trouble from tomorrow—I intended to make more tonight.

I glanced at the watch on my wrist. Nine-thirty. In another hour the riff-raff of Newport would be crawling out of their cocoons. They would head straight for the places the pleasure-bent went on a Sunday night. They would mix with the innocent pleasure-seekers, make new acquaintances, butter up old. All for the money in their pockets.

I stubbed my cigarette out, finished the beer. The beer whetted my appetite. I didn't want to eat in the sterile, white kitchen. I checked my wallet; hundred and forty-four, plus some change in my pocket and the key to the 'Bird. My hand was on the doorknob. I paused.

After eating, I was going to the Barby. Big John would there, with the other menials and jackals he commanded. If I wanted a heart to heart talk with him, I had to take care of the menials and jackals first. One man I'll handle, without killing him. Two or more, regardless of strength, no one man can handle, without killing or crippling. I wasn't ready to kill or cripple. Not yet.

I went into my bedroom and got some white power, put it in an envelope.

CHAPTER FIVE

PARKED THE 'BIRD IN FRONT OF THE RESTAURANT. I found a table against the wall, between two of the indirect lighting fixtures. Looking over the menu, I decided on broiled steak, with mushrooms and a little dry wine. The chair on the side of my table scraped back with a whispering sound. A heavy, corpulent bulk settled into it. I raised my eyes from the menu.

Detective Sergeant James Hogarth, Vice Squad. It was the officer that had hauled Big John, Tim, Jackson, and me into the night police court last night.

"Do'ye mind?" asked Hogarth. "Got a little something to say to you."

"Can it wait?"

He closed his lips, popped breath through them. " 'Fraid not. You'll be in front of Judge Samuels tomorrow at nine. Too late then. Been looking for you all afternoon."

"Yeah?" There went any alibis I might have used for the time of Sheila's murder.

"Order your meal. Don't want anything myself." He waved a thick hand at the waitress, coming up to the table.

I ordered, crisply, quietly. "Bring the Sergeant a Vodka," I said. "No smell, no taste. A nice lift without penalty," I said to Hogarth, who started to wave it down. His eyes fastened on mine.

"Okay," he grunted.

He sat at the table, said nothing, letting the silence build. A dumb looking cop, I thought but probably smart. He had all the

training the skull-shrinkers can give a flat-foot in this enlight-
ened twentieth century. Ponderous law, setting quiet, make a
man sweat, squirm, build up a tension. The waitress brought the
order, placed it efficiently, left. I cut the steak, stabbed it with my
fork.

"Fair warning," I said. "If you sit there looking at me when I
start eating, you're going to need that Vodka. When I eat, my face
looks like I'm chewing on it, not the steak."

"Know all about it," he grunted.

I lowered the fork and piece of steak carefully back to the
plate.

"Yeah?"

"Yeah," Hogarth said. "Been wondering about you. About
birds and bees that have been buzzing and chirping about your
counseling business. Been wondering since you set up shop two
months ago. Had no chance to check, until last night. Thanks for
drinking that glass of water I gave you at the courthouse."

"Fingerprints, huh?"

"Yeah." Got the report this morning. Also got a call from
some doctor, up at a Naval Hospital. Seems they're keeping a tab
on you."

"What?" That hadn't been in the bargain, not when I left the
hospital. I was to be a free agent. Report back in six months. Call
a number, if anything happened before then. They wanted to
be sure that I became acclimated to society without too much
trouble.

"Not following you or anything," Hogarth continued. "Just
have the fingerprint section alerted, in case anything comes in
on you. This doctor thought he had better talk to the local police,
since the charge was assault and disorderly conduct. Said he was
Doctor S-l-n-e-a-d-i." Hogarth spelled the name. "Sounded like
he said it was slide and die. Voice sounded foreign like."

"Eurasian. Chinese," I said to his unasked question. "Seems like China has a few people in it like me. He's still checking."

"Must be hell," Hogarth said.

"Mind if I eat? Turn your face away, if you want."

"Don't worry about me. Seen faces smeared on windshields, sidewalks, with broken beer bottles, the works."

"Okay. Like the program says: you asked for it."

I put the steak in my mouth, started chewing.

"Yeah!" Hogarth snorted, suddenly harsh. "First I'll tell you what that Doc Slide and Die said. He said that if you ever went off your rocker, not to try to get close to you. That no straitjacket would hold you, even if we could get one on. He said to use a gun on you—preferably a high-powered rifle—so we wouldn't have to get too close. Put the bullet in your head. One in the body wouldn't stop you quick enough." He glanced at me, saw that I was eating, looked hastily away. "Nice guy, that doc, turning you loose on society."

"I've got all my marbles," I snapped. "Probably more than some thickset, sloppy cop I know. They let him run around in society."

"Okay. Okay. So you got all your marbles. The doc said so. But he added that if society rejects you finally and completely—whatever that means—you might lose them, all at once. Go berserk." Hogarth looked at me again, saw that I was still eating. He closed his eyes, downed the Vodka.

"Stop that gawddamned face-making so I can talk to you!" he half-shouted, then looked flustered. "Sorry, but it is awful."

I put down the fork.

"I didn't invite you to this table," I said coldly. "You can leave when you want. By the way, the crack you just made about my 'face-making'; things like that is what the doc meant when he said society might reject me. Some little thing like that might make me go berserk—suddenly."

"I said I'm sorry." Hogarth looked harried. "But what I want has nothing to do with your face. That fight the other night—I know it was about gambling. I also know that you picked up a lot of money." He held up his hand when I started to interrupt. "No, I can't prove it, damnit. That's what I want you to do. Tell the judge tomorrow. It'll make it easy on you and I'll close that place so quick they won't have time to clean the stale beer up on the bar."

"You telling me you can stop gambling? You're the nut, not me."

Hogarth looked at me grimly. "I can try," he snapped.

I leaned forward, looked him in the eye. He pulled back from the glare in mine. I picked up a spoon, put the handle between thumb and finger.

"*I'm* going to break up this gambling racket. You ask how? Like I'm rolling up this spoon." I held the spoon up in front of his startled eyes, rolling it up like a stick of chewing gum before you pop it in your mouth, until the dish part flattened out and made a tight ball. "Use brute strength, use anything I have to use, but I'm going to nail the one person holding it together. Or they're going to kill me first, with a broken neck, an accident. If I'm found dead, think of that, Sergeant. Think of that!" I threw the spoon on the table. "I'm not doing it for you, or John Q. Public, or anybody else. I'm doing it for Kirk. Kirkpatrick—James. Does that mean anything to you? Hell, no. How could it? He was just the punk that fell off the Boat Club upper deck, accidentally drowned with a broken neck!

"Now get the hell out of here and let me eat, flatfoot." I picked up the knife and fork, cut the cold steak.

Hogarth got slowly to his feet.

"If you do anything, if you flip your lid, I'm coming looking for you, with a high-powered rifle."

"Bring the high-powered rifle. Bring it by all means," I said. I could feel his eyes on me for a moment, before he said slowly, "The law is the law, Mr. Todd. If I ever have to order the rifles on you, I'll make damn sure there is no other way first."

CHAPTER SIX

I PARKED THE 'BIRD OFF YORK STREET, on Seventh, in a no parking zone. I might need the car in a hurry and maneuvering from between bumper to bumper parked cars might cancel the margin of safety. The hands of my watch pointed to a few minutes past ten. I stepped into the barroom of the Barby Cafe, looked the barroom crowd over.

The barroom is long and narrow. As you come in, the bar is on your left, a jukebox almost blocking the doorway. In back of the jukebox a few tables are crowded against the wall. At the far end on the bar side, the original partition has been cut out, forming a large entrance. Through that entrance, in the two large rooms in back, are the gambling tables.

The barroom was thick with stale air and smoke, and two bartenders were busy slopping out the poison to the crowd jammed on the bar stools. Girls in tight dresses, girls in blue jeans, with tight, transparent blouses, the almost transparent bra's showing through the thin material, occupied the stools. You needed only a glance to know that the girls that wore dresses had nothing on under them, made it cooler that way—as well as faster and easier.

Not a man was bellied up to the bar. They were busy at the back room, trying to win some money for the chicks out front.

I wedged myself into the crowd of soft bodies at the bar, ordered a scotch and soda. The girls turned, looked me over, some with calculating interest. The one that I was wedged against on my right smiled up into my face, showing even, white teeth.

Her eyes had the smoky look. A lot of young girls are learning to wear it permanently.

"Hi, Doll," she said with gamin frankness. "Don't mind digging your elbow into my personalities when you lift your drink. They are soft—they give easy."

"Thanks, Beautiful." I smiled at her with my eyes. "Bet there is a lot of you that gives easily."

"What is a gal to do when she runs into a hard thing?" she flipped with a grin. "Anybody knows that soft things can't stop hard things. She has to give or get bruised."

I'd heard it before. Had ignored it before. But since those few minutes with Sheila in the willows, my body was re-awakened to the pleasures only a girl can offer—and give. To take this girl for a ride, to take this girl for fun, all I had to do was slip my fingers around her soft elbow and lead her out to the car. She saw the indecision in my eyes.

"Not ready yet, Doll?" she asked mockingly. "Go on back and buck the tables for awhile. If you don't lose all your dough, I'l be waiting."

Keep on waiting, I thought, and turned my back to the bar, the drink in my hand. As I raised the drink to my lips, over the rim of the glass my eyes fastened on another pair of eyes, the owner sitting alone at one of the tables against the wall.

Those eyes were large and brown and soft. So soft that I felt myself sinking down into them. They held onto mine, until I tipped the glass up. When I brought the empty glass down, the girl was sitting looking at the stained tablecloth. Not girl. Woman.

Her black hair was long and curly, tied carelessly up with what looked like a cheap rhinestone tiara into what would have been a ponytail—if the hair wasn't so curly. It spilled all over in back of the tiara in a soft casade of swoops and swirls. Two large butterflies were pinned to her ears, glistening and sparkling. Her profile, with tilted nose, full lips, soft rounded chin, was piquant. The sooty black hair, with the sooty black eyebrows, caused the pearl-white of her skin on her throat and face to take on the etched look of a fine cameo.

My eyes swept down the white summer dress, over the bumps and hollows to the small waist, the full hips resting lightly on the chair, the rounded legs ending in small high-heeled shoes. One, which was kicked slightly loose, hung on the toes of the one foot crossed over the ankle.

"Not that, Doll." The girl at my right had turned half around, was following my look. "That can't be had. Comes in and sits around, drinking it straight. She'll throw the glass in your face if you make a pass."

"Yeah?"

"Yeah," she said. "That's not dime store stuff she's wearing. See those rings on her fingers? Diamonds, Doll." The beauty at the table had her hands wrapped around her drink glass, was staring moodily into it.

"Nice joint to wear diamonds in. Some of these punks will lift them, sure as hell," I remarked idly.

"Looks like they would. Never heard of anyone trying to. Funny." She looked at the girl at the table speculatively. "Course, she always comes in a cab. Leaves in one, too. I've seen her in other joints. Say, what am I doing? Helping you make a pitch for that? Look, honey, there's plenty of good stuff closer to you than that. Probably could be had, too." Her eyes were bold, no more dodging or doubting.

"The gambling rooms in back, remember?" I said lightly. "Wait and see if I have any money when I come out."

"Don't worry about the money, Doll," she called after me as I started for the entrance to the back rooms. "I'm the kind of gal that'll trust a man like you."

I couldn't help but to take one more look at the girl sitting at the table. She looked up, full into my eyes. She smiled, a tiny, wistful smile, just the corners of her full lips moving. For a second I hated the chore I had, hated the thought of the path of destruction I was on. Damn the girls! I said bleakly to myself, walking lightly through the entrance into the first of the game rooms.

The roulette table was getting a good play. The Blackjack—or 21—table had a few hungry men bucking it. Chuckaluc was taking a good play, but it was small time, twenty-five, fifty cent bets. Now and then a dollar fluttered. Betting would grow as the evening wore on, the drinks making the players reckless with the rent money.

Big John wasn't in the first room. I hadn't expected him there. He would be in the next room. Cards. Straight dice. Higher stakes.

I eased into the next room, pushed back against the wall by the doorway. I didn't know what Big John would do when he saw me. I didn't much care. When I got the chance, Big John was going to be a mighty sick man.

I spotted him at the big card table. His right arm was in a sling, a cigar sticking in his oily puss, thick lips worrying it. He held his cards in his left hand, laid them down to sort and pick discards. The other two punks, Tim and Jackson, were over with the dice crowd, bouncing them down the long board. I kept my eyes on Big John. He was boss man here. I noticed his shot glass was empty. A short flouncy waitress kept moving around, picking up empties, taking orders. She picked up his glass.

I saw him nod his head. The waitress came hurrying by me, went out to the bar, tray stacked with empties. I palmed the big envelope, got a five dollar bill out of my wallet, waited.

The waitress came hurrying back. She had about a dozen drinks perched on the tray. As she came through the door, I stepped in front of her.

"How about a scotch and soda?" I said.

"Sure. Let me serve these drinks."

"Hell no! I been trying to catch you for twenty minutes. You get to moving around in that crowd again and I'll never get a drink. Here, I'll hold the tray." I stuck the five-spot under her nose. "All for one scotch and soda—and better service later on?" I said softly.

"Five dollars—for one drink?" she was startled.

"I'm watching a play. Don't want to miss it. Doing a little figuring on the eight passes on the long board," I said impatiently. "Well, do you want this fiver or not?"

I took hold of the tray, shoved the bill into her greedy little paw.

"Okay," she said. "Don't spill the drinks.…" and was off for the bar, her buttocks bouncing with her half-walk, half-run.

I faced the wall, tore the envelope open with my teeth. Eleven drinks were on the tray. I poured a like amount into each drink. A little more than was necessary. Palming the envelope, I turned facing the doorway as the flouncy waitress came charging in. She slipped the drink into my hand, took the tray.

"Thanks," she said.

"Thank you," I said fervently.

Big John got one of the glasses. Tim and Jackson each got one. I'd noticed it the other evening: When Big John ordered, he ordered for all three, else the other two didn't drink. I watched Tim and Jackson look towards Big John, tip their drinks to him. Big John tipped his back. I didn't care what other suckers got one of the drinks. That would create a diversion.

Chloral hydrate works fast. I didn't have long to wait. I saw the sweat break out on Big John's face, the sudden chalk-white of his oily, olive skin. Tim and Jackson were developing the same symptoms. Chloral hydrate is rough stuff. Take a balloon and squeeze it in the middle. Notice how the air rushed to both ends? That's what chloral hydrate does to your stomach; squeezes it in the middle and whatever is in there rushes both ways, violently. It's impossible to get both ends in the john at the same time. It also makes the room go round and round, so that it is even hard to find the john. One second you're freezing, the next burning up, limp as a used dishrag. One time in your life when you want to die and are afraid that you won't.

The door to the john was a normal size door. The eleven men that ran and staggered and lurched to it couldn't all get in.

I grabbed Big John in the uproar, swung him around like a used wet mop and hauled him through the side door. I pushed, shoved and slapped him several buildings up the alley, dumped him over a low fence into a back yard. He was groaning and cursing, so I put my shoe in his mouth. But I had to jerk it out when he vomited. Then I put it back in.

"Oh, gawd," he groaned around the shoe.

CHAPTER SEVEN

REACHED DOWN AND SLAPPED HIS FACE, taking my shoe out of his bleeding mouth. Back and forth I slapped that oily face, hard.

"You're going to talk, damn you, or I'll do worse than break that other arm." I was breathing hard. Fighting down the memory of Sheila, of Kirk. A memory that started a flame burning in me, that made me want to rip and tear and shred, not question. "Who works for your gang that wears a black and white checkered sports-coat? Big muscle-bound bruiser—what's the murdering bastard's name?"

Big John gagged, got rid of a sour mouthful. Taking a shuddering breath, he looked into my face hanging over him and tried to squirm away.

"I asked you a question, damn you!" I knocked his head sideways on the ground with the driving palm of my hand. "I'll get answers or I'll take you apart, piece by piece."

"You mean Mule? What the hell you want with Mule?" he groaned, got rid of some more.

"Where can I find him? Where does he hang out?"

"The Boat Club," Big John said sullenly. "That's his territory. What the hell you want with him?"

The Boat Club. Kirk. Off the upper deck. Broken neck. Sheila—broken neck. My stomach started quivering.

"You greasy sonofabitch," I rasped, rage choking in my throat. "What do you know about Sheila Thomson? Give, you greasy bastard! Or so help me, I'll mash your ugly face into the ground." I put my foot into his face, put part of my hundred eighty-three pounds on it.

"My girl," he croaked.

"Your girl!" I spat through locked teeth. "Forcing her to make bed money? Tricking her to lose money so she has to shack up with every lousy bum you want her to? You lying, greasy pig!" I put my heel on his thick ear, twisted it.

"Huh?" he wheezed.

"Huh, hell. Spill it!" I kicked him hard in the gut, put my heel back on his ear. He grabbed at it with his free hand.

"Keep that filthy paw off me, or I'll grind your ear off. You're not dealing with some cop that can't afford to rough you up, that can't even open your mouth with an arrest warrant, you gutter-rooting pig. I asked you about Sheila."

He took his hand from my ankle, half-groaned, half-sobbed. He vomited again.

"Sheila's my girl. She don't have to shack up with anybody. I'd kill the bastard that shacked up with her." He got some breath, started talking in a rush. "Whoever told you that is lying. I wouldn't even let her gamble. I give her all the money she wants."

"She doesn't have to have any of your filthy money, not where she's at now!"

"I know, I know," he said, choking on more vomit. "I heard it on the radio. I—I don't know why—I can't think of any reason for it. Maybe it was a—a sex louse."

"You don't know!" I jeered. "Ask your boss. Ask the boss man or woman. I'd love to be with you when you ask. What would you do, you tin horn crook? What would you do if the boss said sure, that she had got in the road?"

"If she did something she shouldn't, I guess she had it coming," he said sullenly.

Rage boiled up in a choking frenzy within me. I stomped his ear, ground on it, wanting to mash the head under it.

"What kind of a man you call yourself?" I asked through my rage tightening throat. "Even a dog will fight for his bitch when she's in heat! It's no use telling you that your friend Mule did it. Not a damn bit of use. You'll shake his hand for it and buy him a drink."

"How do you know Mule did it?" he asked weakly.

"Because I was there. I was there when he broke her neck, you hyena. He tried to break mine, too. If I decide you had anything directly to do with it, you'll only have two seconds to live after I get my hands on you. Got that, you stinking gob of spineless flesh? Two lousy damned seconds. But why let you live any longer? What the hell you good for?" I kicked him in the head, raised my foot high over his head. "What in the hell is to stop me mashing your head like I would a snake's? You got anything worthwhile to say that might make me change my mind, that might make me decide that there is some reason for letting the breath stay in that worthless hide of yours?"

Meanness was boiling through me. I could feel it tearing at the roots of my mind. The intensity of it suddenly scared me. I actually wanted him to get nasty, or stay sullen, so that I could go on stomping him. I lowered my foot slowly, forcing it down, fighting for control. I took a deep breath, felt my insides loosening up.

"You going to level with me?" I asked quietly.

The quietness of my voice scared him more than my snarling had. He tried to drag himself away with his one hand, the broken arm in the cast flopping helplessly. He had to stop to vomit.

I waited until he quit gagging.

"Well?"

"So help me, gawd," he half-sobbed. "I'm leveling. Sheila was my girl. She didn't have to shack up with anyone. She was a nice kid. I liked her. Hell, I was even thinking of marrying her."

His voice had the ring of truth. He was too scared, too sick from the drug to be thinking up lies.

"Who's your boss? The one who gave orders to kill Sheila? Kill me? Talk, rat. You're not far from dying. Not yet. Who is your boss?" I was keeping my voice low, deadly, with an effort.

"I don't know," he said sullenly.

"That won't keep you alive. Where do you get your stake money from, tin-horn?" I snapped it at him.

"From the bank," he blurted it. "So help me, I don't know who deposits it in my name."

"What name you use to draw the money from the bank? Your own?"

"No." He went sullen again. The drug was wearing off. I heard the dismal wail of sirens heading our way. Probably a first class riot in the Barby. Big John heard them, too.

"The police can't keep you from dying. I've got two, three minutes yet. What name do you use?" He didn't answer. I kicked him in the face. Hard. "What name? I might need it for your tombstone."

"It's a code name," he said, his breath blowing blood from his mouth.

"Quit stalling! What name?" I kicked him in the gut.

"George Jones," he gasped. The sirens were close.

"You put your winnings back in under the same name?"

"Go to hell," he snarled, taking courage from the nearness of the police cars.

I stomped him in the face. "For bad manners," I said savagely. "I asked you a question."

"Yes," he blubbered.

"Any idea of your own who the boss is? Quick, or so help me, I'll kick your head loose from your spine!" When dealing with pigs, you kill them at harvest time. This was my harvest time. These pigs had been fattening on the corn of suckers for a long time, on the corn and blood of suckers. I felt no pity, only contempt with a sickening rage. Wallowing in the same muck with them, even if it was for Kirk, brought the gall to my mouth, tinged the hate with bitterness.

Big John was enough of the gambler to sense the emotions boiling in me. Through the haze of his sick stomach and dazed brain, he suddenly saw through me to the naked savage. His oily face, smeared with blood and dirt, went paper white in the night shadows. He started shaking, the whole blubbery mass of him.

"Who do you think it is? For the last time." I put my toe against the base of his head, marking the exact spot, swung it slowly back.

"I never tried to find out! Nobody asks questions about the boss! Anyone that did, they don't last long. Oh, gawd—please!" he squealed it out in a sudden frenzy, seeing my foot driving for his head.

A fraction of a second before finality, the lust to kill was overcome by the uselessness of it. I turned the driving toe from the base of his head, let the heel smash into the slack jaw.

His head snapped around, smeared into his vomit. My body started an involuntary trembling, rage draining off and leaving me chilled. I noticed the blood on my brown oxford. I took the bottom half of Big John's coat and almost gently wiped it clean, hearing his breath blubbering in and out of his bloody lips.

CHAPTER EIGHT

THE SIRENS WERE DYING TO A THROATY SOB as I came out of the alley on seventh street, a few short steps away from my parked 'Bird. As I came around the corner of the building, a huge shadow broke away from the wall, stood ponderously alert, moved towards me as I put my hand on the door handle of the car.

"Roscoe Todd?" the voice rumbled in his deep chest.

I looked up at him towering over me. At the oversize, round skull, the broad flat face, seemingly made small by the tree-trunk dimensions of his throat.

"What do you want?" I asked sharply, already knowing.

"Nothing," he rumbled. "I got my money. I only got the job to do before I catch the next train back to Chi. Don't make it hard for me and I'll go easy on you." He reached one ham-sized hand out, clamping it on my left shoulder.

"Hey!" I yelped. "What's it all about? Let me know the reason why you want to obviously beat my brains out. What's your name?"

"The letter I got says you'll know the reason why—I don't, fella. All I know is that I'll get to keep the ten C's that was in it."

"You got the letter with you?" I asked swiftly. Letters can be traced, up to a point, by any citizen.

"Aw, hell, fella" he said impatiently. "What'ta I wanta keep the letter for? Now you take it easy and I won't muss you up too bad. And don't you worry none—I've never killed a job yet."

His hand tightened on my shoulder. He raised his right fist club-like and chopped it down at my upturned face. I caught the fist in my left hand, every joint in my body creaking as I poured the counter muscle to it. For what seemed seconds the fist came ruthlessly down, then slowed to a stop, both our arms quivering from the exertion.

"What the hell?" he muttered in perplexion. His mind worked too slow to grasp the situation. Irritated, he jerked his fist from my cupped hand.

Jungle law doesn't allow for retreat.

I shot my left hand, fingers splayed, into his eye sockets. Felt the wetness and blubber under his eye-balls. His left hand loosed the numbing grip in my shoulder, freed my right arm. I shot a vicious right-cross to his chin, stepped back. Then I dug my hand into my pocket came out with my handkerchief, wrapped it around my right hand, and closed the hand into a cement hard fist.

"You crazy sonofabitch!" he bellowed, rubbing his lacerated eyes. "I'll break you in little pieces for this!"

He came at me, huge arms outstretched, pawing for me in his near blindness.

I stepped inside those huge arms, buried my weight into the cement, put all the power I had a singing right-cross to his jaw, just below the ear. The impact numbed my arm to the shoulder, the tightly wrapped handkerchief kept my hand from busting like an over-ripe tomato.

He turned half around, shuffled awkwardly across the side-walk, arms still pawing in front of his body, bumped into the brick wall of the brick building.

I shook the handkerchief from my numbed hand, rubbed some feeling back into it. More police cars were beating a wailing path to the door of the Barby, making the night eerie with the unhuman sound of the sirens. Safety was distance for me, right now. But I wasn't sure if my gargantuan friend had had enough. I didn't want him ripping the door off the 'Bird as I pulled away from the curb. He was showing signs of coming out of the shock of my blow.

I decided to finish the job, to give him enough so he wouldn't come looking for me again.

I stepped swiftly across the walk, grabbed him by the ankles and jerked both feet out from under him. His face made a rasping sound as it cascaded down the rough brick wall, then squished as it hit the pavement. I stomped him in the lower spine and kidneys, making sure his back would be sore enough to keep him out of his dirty business for a month. I drove the toe of my brown oxford into the sore spot on his jaw, watched his squirming body relax. Slowly I bent down and listened to make sure he was still breathing. He was.

I gunned the 'Bird away from the curb. Down seventh to Isabelle, down Isabelle to the river front, a savage satisfaction tingling my senses. After two months I was starting to move in the direction of the gambling boss. I had ceased to be a minor nuisance and had become a major threat—and a candidate for a hospital ward.

The last of the sirens were dying to an echo as I whipped the 'Bird into a parking slot at the Boat Club. I wasn't worried about Big John. Not any more. He was scared. If the police found him lying there in his vomit, he wouldn't know who it was that worked him over. His was the breed. He'd vow to himself to even things. Dream about the beating he was going to give me. About how he would send me screaming to hell. But it would be tomorrow. Always tomorrow.

It was interesting to know how the boss worked with the tinhorns. The boss could put in and take out what he wanted from the bank. All he—or she—needed was the signature card. His name and the code name. Joint accounts. The boss would draw money from one bank to another. Draft it all over the country, from Maine to California. Slick. If the tin-horn took out money and didn't put it back, word was passed to some thugs—how I didn't know yet, probably by telephone—and the tin-horn got his lumps.

True, the tin-horn could get serious about knowing who his boss was. He could demand to see the card, or use some excuse to get his hands on it. But the boss could also use other names. And Big John said that it was unhealthy to even think about who the boss was.

But I was up a great big alley, dead end. There was no way that I could check banks. Even if I got one of the signature cards, you don't get any information out of a bank. Not unless you have a writ from the courthouse.

Beating up the muscle men and the tin-horns wasn't going to get me the information. They didn't know. It could get me killed, or jailed. The big bruiser from Chicago—now lying on the sidewalk on Seventh Street—was the first direct move against me. I couldn't count the murder at Tacoma. The thugs had gone for Sheila first. Why, I didn't know. I was probably a side item, then. If they overheard Sheila offering to spill her guts to me, had heard her name some names and reported it to the boss, then I was a definite target. Hence the bruiser on Seventh Street.

The gang ruled by muscle. So their first thought would be more muscle. So they hauled in almost a quarter-ton of it. Now the quarter-ton of beef was nothing but stew meat. I wasn't waiting for their next move.

No, the boss couldn't take pressure. I intended to put the pressure on. Beat and scare his men, scare them right down to the bottom of their filthy pants. Where they lived. The boss would have to keep moving, have to stop me. He'd have to mash me and then blot me from the streets of Newport. If it was a he. Somehow the set-up smelled like a woman. A clever, heartless, scheming, maybe beautiful woman.

I walked across the catwalk to the Boat Club, black Ohio River water under me. The same black water Kirk plunged into. Mule hung out here, so Big John said. I was looking for Mule. Whoever Mule was. He wore a black and white checkered sportscoat and had a badly bitten finger. Maybe I couldn't get the boss, but I could get Mule. Mule was undoubtedly the man that got Kirk. That was what I was here for: to get the man that got Kirk. If I could get his boss—good. If I died before I got to the boss, with Mule going to hell first, then I would die feeling good. Haven't really felt good since 1942—or was it '43? Been feeling really lousy since 1956. When I paid Kirk's funeral bill. I shook it off.

The Boat Club is a large boathouse with a catwalk around it. Little jetties sticking out into the black water with pleasure boats roped tight. The money don't come from the dock fees. The dock fees made it legal. Just like the 'club' part made closing hours on whisky and beer mean absolutely nothing. A club can serve as long as a member is present. As I walked in the door to the first deck part of the club, I was made a member.

"Twenty-five cents," said the faded blond at the cash register. "Unless you are already a member?"

"Not a member," I said, handing her the money. She gave me a ticket from a big roll by the cash register.

"What do I do with this?" I asked blankly.

"Keep it to use again. Or give it to a waitress. She'll give you credit for it on your drinks," the faded blond answered in a bored voice, already back to her faded dreams, probably about Hollywood.

I looked the boat over. The air was at least fresh. The river breeze blew the cigaret smoke away. Tables, chairs, bar, small dance floor, jukebox. The place was about half filled. Men and women. Boys and girls. Tight dresses. Tight blue jeans. The same: Barby's, The Aces, Mike's. Same bodies, different faces stuck on top. My eyes found the stairway to the second deck. Also the two hundred and fifty pounds of beef standing at the foot of them. I walked over, put my foot on the first step.

"Not regular here, are ya, pal?" the beef asked.

"So?"

"So what do you want up there?"

"Whatever is up there."

The beef looked at me. I looked at the beef. "I dunno," he said. "Dunno to let you up or not."

"Going to stop me?"

"Oh, hell, go on. You look all right to me." He turned his back.

I went up.

The action was here. The long board. Blackjack. You name it. The Boat Club has it. But strictly third rate, dimes and quarters. But enough dimes and quarters add up. Add up to dollars, thousand of dollars.

I couldn't help but see her. I started to look for a white and black checkered sportscoat. All I saw was her. She saw me, too. Else why was she moving that tawny body through the thick crowd toward me. She cleared the crowd and kept right on coming. Her pantherish, tawny body as graceful as a cat. But a cat never had bumps in front the way she had. Nor is a cat sheathed in a gold lame dress. Lame? To mix the word, if that dress was lame, then I'm a hopeless cripple. Healthy, seductive movements, all over it. She had to have green eyes. She did.

"Slumming?" she asked, her eyelashes half-hiding her green eyes, a small smile curving the thick, sensual lips. She didn't stop the sliaking walk until her bumpers were almost rubbing my coat lapels.

"Could ask the same of you," I answered.

"Are you?"

"Am I what?"

"Asking the same of me?"

"Yes. Slumming?" I asked, letting my eyes smile.

"Hmmmmm." She looked me over critically. "If I am, what are you going to do about it?"

"What am I supposed to do about it?"

"I'm hungry," she said. "I'd like to eat some sauerkraut Sauerkraut and wieners."

"Now wait a minute—" I began.

"Oh, you don't know me," she said brightly. "In the snob class we are supposed to be introduced. I'll introduce myself. I'm Barbara Medina."

"Roscoe Todd. At your service." I made a mock bow.

"Delighted," she murmured. I expected her to offer me her hand to kiss. Instead she smiled, showing slightly crooked, but white, broad teeth.

"Shall we have the sauerkraut and wieners?" She took my arm. "I know just the place."

CHAPTER NINE

"I'M HERE ON BUSINESS," I said flatly.

"Oh?"

"Yes. I'm looking for someone."

"Your wife?"

"Haven't got one. Looking for a man named Mule."

"Mule? Did you say Mule? Must be quite a character."

"Yeah. He usually wears a black and white checkered sportscoat. Seen him around?"

"Oh, you mean that character! Runs the gambling or something, doesn't he?"

"Know quite a lot, don't you?"

"I've been here before. Fun watching the working man lose his last dollar. They have a fight once in awhile. Gee, is that fun!"

"Not for the guy involved," I said.

"Boxers don't think it's fun, either, but they do it." She laughed, an intimate, teasing laugh.

I decided to ignore it. This feather-headed dame was on the make. Later, maybe, but not now. I wanted Mule.

"Have you seen that character around?" I asked.

"That character? No, he's not been here tonight. There's another guy here running the show. See him over there?"

I looked where she was pointing. The guy was about five ten, maybe a hundred fifty pounds, blond hair, sharp featured face. He grinned in short, nervous starts and stops, talking to some old man with a fistful of green-backs. It was strictly a friendly conversation.

"Well?" asked Barbara.

"Well what?"

"Do I get my sauerkraut and wieners?"

"You certainly have a one-track mind, Barbara."

"Make it Barby. Yes, but one-track minds can be nice, can't they? If they get switched on the right track?" She looked up into my eyes, lips slightly parted, eyes veiled. "Right now, I'm riding the train for sauerkraut and wieners. When I get to the end of that track, I can switch easy and do something both of us might like to do."

I smiled with my eyes at the teasing implication. Her light, buoyant mood was catching. Her open, headlong flirting made me suspicious; she could be one of the gang. She also could be one of those girls with nothing to do, bored with her everyday life of luxury, out for the kicks.

Mule wasn't here. I couldn't very well go chasing him over three cities. If I found him anywhere, it would probably be here. If he was holed up somwhere, nursing his finger, my evening was free. Unless I wanted to bust up a few gambling places, just on general principle.

If Barby was a member of the gang—so what? I was taking on all comers, wasn't I? I looked at my wristwatch. This was one 'comer' I would enjoy taking on—or off. The clothes, that is.

"And just where can we find sauerkraut and wieners at this time of the night? It's five of eleven."

"Beverly Hills," Barby said. "You can get anything at Beverly Hills." She smiled wickedly.

"Anything?" I tried to put the proper nuance in the question.

"That—," she said, tapping my chest with a slender finger, "—you bring with you. If you are real nice, Beverly Hills will help put it in the mood to go home with you—your home."

"Beverly Hills sounds like a nice place for men with good girls and naughty ideas," I said, smiling with my eyes. I wanted to see Beverly Hills, sort of look it over. Sheila had mentioned a connection there. "Shall we go?" I asked, offering my arm.

"We shall go," she said gaily, taking my arm and tucking it under hers, close against one of the swelling bumps. "March on the sauerkraut and wieners. Forwar—oops, the steps!"

We went down the steps, her weight resting lightly against me, causing her hip to rub mine gently. The jukebox was going when we hit the first deck and she slipped her arms around my neck, danced me whirling across the small floor, out to the door.

"Fun," she said, throwing her arms wide. "I like fun!"

Detective Sergeant James Hogarth stood just outside the door. His pale eyes were fastened on me.

"Thought you were here. Saw your car," he grunted.

"Better get another car. The bloodhounds have the scent," I said, watching him.

Barby was watching both of us.

"Know anything about what happened up at the Barby?" Hogarth asked.

"Should I?"

"Didn't think you would," he said sarcastically. "Been here long?"

"Hours and hours," Barby chirped. "Broke all the games. So if you're a cop, trying to pick up some money, you're too late. We got it all." She laughed saucily in his face.

Hogarth frowned.

"I can't stop you, you been here that long. Going far?"

"We're trying for the moon," Barby said flippantly. "But we'll settle for Beverly Hills. If you got any money, you can come along." She looked at his rumpled suit, the sweat-soaked collar. "On second sight—don't come along. They wouldn't let us in."

"So long as you're in court tomorrow, I don't care where you go," he grunted. "In case you're curious, they had a nice riot up at the Barby. Somebody mickied a bunch of drinks. Two guys looked like a truck had run them down."

Two guys? At the Barby? They must have found the gorilla from Chicago on Seventh Street. Un-huh, Hogarth was trying to be clever.

"What did the two guys do—get in a fight?" I asked innocently.

"But not with each other," Hogarth said pointedly. "They were too far apart. But you wouldn't know about that." He obviously had put two and two together and had surprisingly come up with four.

"Proof, Officer. You must have proof," I said lightly.

"Or a warrant," he said. "Or maybe I'm hoping one of those guys might die. On murder I'd really be able to handle things my way," he ended flatly, turned on his heel and clumped heavily across the catwalk.

"What a creature," Barby said. "He was a cop, wasn't he?"

"Yes. Vice Squad. You got a license?"

She made a round O with her lips, opened her eyes wide.

"Mommy didn't tell me that I needed one for that," she said. "Mommy said I only needed a license when I married it."

This girl was impossible.

"Aren't you going to ask me what he wanted with me? Not even why I have to be in court tomorrow? You might be stepping out with a pretty mean character."

"You met me three minutes ago and already you expect me to start acting like a wife?" She grinned impishly.

"Why did you tell him that I was here for hours and hours?"

"Didn't you have a Mommy?" She tossed her shoulder-length copper hair. "Mommy said to never tell the truth to cops."

"What if he had asked you if you were a good girl?"

"I would lie to him," she said demurely. "I'd tell him that I was a bad girl."

"Hmmmm," I hummed.

"Come on," she laughed, took me by the arm. "Take me out to Beverly Hills, stuff me with sauerkraut and wieners, let them work on me. See whose home I go to afterwards." She looked up at me out of the corner of her eye. "That's the way to get your question answered. You maybe played cops and robbers yesterday, you can play them again tomorrow, but tonight, I've elected you my man. All my men are always nice to me." She made it a statement. "Maybe it's because I'm always nice to them," she whispered throatily.

CHAPTER TEN

HEADED THE 'BIRD OUT OF TOWN, driving south on Saratoga Street. Barby was snuggled close, head on my shoulder, her coppery, softly waved hair tickling my ear and neck. The heavy musk of her perfume caused my pulses to throb. She raised her left hand, stroked the left side of my face gently, let her fingers travel up and mix lightly with my short curly hair.

"Hey?" I said softly. "Want me to wreck the car?"

"No, Darling," she said in a humming voice. "It's going to take us out to Beverly, remember? Where they can go to work on me, soften me up…. this is a Thunderbird Sporter, isn't it? Never rode in one before. Bet it will go."

"How much you bet?" I asked huskily. She laughed softly.

"I like to play games. Games of chance," she whispered against my ear. "After you leave the last stoplight on Alexandria Pike, you can put your hand on my leg, two inches above the knee. As long as you hold the gas pedal to the floor, you can move your hand six inches a minute, until we get to Beverly Hills. I'm betting the car will move faster than your hand."

"I might cheat!"

"Not you, Darling," she said. "Besides, I'll have my hand on yours—and my foot on top of yours on the gas pedal."

"I'm calling that bet!" I said as we flashed under the last stoplight. She picked my hand from the steering-wheel, slipped it under her dress above her knee.

"Let's go!" she breathed into my ear. I felt one of the gold sandals jam down on top of mine.

The 'Bird did a screaming half-circle as the tires fought the blacktop for a hold, then snapped our heads back and rammed us into the cushions.

"One minute!" Barby said, her voice shaking with excitement.

My hand crawled leisurely up her hot, tingling thigh. She stopped it with a gentle pressure of her fingers, snuggled tighter against me. I could feel her heart hammering under the breast tight against my coat sleeve.

I picked up the lights from the top of the hill out of the corner of my eye. Beverly Hills is three miles out of Newport, not counting the driveway to the top of the hill. The driveway, as you leave the highway, is better than a 180 degree turn, making you head back the way you came as you start the quarter mile climb up to the gambling palace.

The turn-off jumped into the headlights, then I was cutting wide on the six lane highway, using it all as no headlights from oncoming cars showed in the soft night I heard Barby gasp, felt her hand bear down on mine, pressing it into the hot flesh.

"Keep that foot on mine!" I said happily. "I like to win my bets."

I swung the wheel hard over, jammed my left foot on the powerful brakes. The tires screamed like fiends in hell; I thought the steering-wheel would come apart in my hand as the front wheels fought to straighten themselves under the terrible pressure. The 'Bird made an agonizing sideslip, the back wheels screaming even with, then past the front. I let up on the brakes and the 'Bird jumped into the turnoff, roared up the drive.

"Better than two minutes!" Barby said, her voice shaking, her hand sliding mine further up the quivering flesh.

ALFRED B. GLASER

I eased on the brake pressure to make a last screaming turn to the left as the drive started its final climb up to and under the portico at the entrance to the gambling palace. Jammed them on with all my weight to bring the car to a grinding stop. Barby took her foot off mine the same instant she said, "Three minutes!"

"Hey!" I yelled as she scrambled out of the car, laughing gaily. "Didn't you forget something?"

"Haven't time to pay off now," she said, sticking her head back in the car. "On the way home, huh?" She wrinkled her nose at me, grinning like an imp.

I turned the car over to the pop-eyed parking attendant.

"Mister," he said, "I dunno 'bout you, but that gal and this car is too beautiful to mangle. You nuts, maybe?"

"It would make you nuts, too, Sonny," I said fervently. "Make you nuts, too," I repeated under my breath as I took Barby's arm and piloted her into the palace.

Beverly Hills is reputed to have cost almost a million dollars to build, back in '37 when a dollar bought a lot. One of the gambling syndicates is said to have backed the builder. True or not, Beverly Hills is one of the most fabulous pleasure barns on the American continent. It brings talent from Hollywood for its floor shows, flies its edibles fresh from place of origin.

As we walked by the check-room, a small cuddly brunette, cigaret tray resting lightly against her bare navel, the rhinestone bra filled out to amazing proportions, leaning one naked hip against the checking counter, made large eyes at me. With a sensuous movement of her hands, arms and hips, she indicated her wares. The ones on the tray and personal. Barby took me firmly by the arm.

"Cigarets I got," she said softly. "Personal belongings I'll match piece for piece and take the bare floor, giving her the sofa for handicap."

50

"No game," I said lightly. "I pride myself on being a man—but not that much of a man!"

Barby looked up at me through her long eyelashes, the green of her eyes cut in half.

"I think it might be fun—," she said wickedly, "—making you prove the first part of what you said."

"The proof is ready and waiting," I replied instantly. "Shall I get the car?"

"Ah, ah! Sauerkraut and wieners, remember?" she said teasingly.

"Shall we grab a stool at the bar?" I asked, indicating the big oval bar, banked with mirrors.

"They don't serve sauerkraut and wieners at the bar," she said with a feigned pout, leading me around the bar toward a solid wall of mirrors. She walked me right into the mirrors. After she stopped I saw the two small chrome handles. I took one and pulled.

Barby slipped through the door and I followed. I glanced behind me and was surprised to see the oval bar through the closed doors. Hollywood stars are too expensive to exhibit for the price of a shot of scotch on the rocks. The barflies had to pay the minimum on a table inside for that. I didn't have time to think too much about the trick mirror. The Maitre de was coming at us with St. Peter's bible.

"Sorry, no reservations," I said, beating him to the question. "I think you could find us something, don't you?" I let him see the edge of the fiver in my hand.

"I believe we have some late cancellations," he lied smoothly.

"I want to sit over there," Barby said promptly, indicating the left side of the ballroom.

"I believe we have a table open on the first tier," the Maitre De acknowledged gratuitously.

"No," Barby said. "I want the second tier. I don't like to sit back where I can't see and I don't want to sit on the dance floor. The second tier—right there." She indicated a table.

The Maitre de succeeded in looking troubled. I dug helplessly for my wallet, fished out a ten. He looked very helpful.

He seated us at the table, swished the reservation sign from sight with a practised flourish, placed fancy drink cards in our hands, beckoned a waiter and retreated to the door, wrapping the fifteen smoothly around the wad he pulled effortlessly from his pocket.

The waiter came up, plump and fortyish, the original Mr. Five by Five. He picked up the gleaming ashtray and polished it vigorously. Setting it down and smoothing the snow white linen table cloth, he flicked imaginary dust from it with his side towel.

"I want sauerkraut and wieners," Barby stated primly.

The seventeen piece orchestra chose that moment to start a number with cymbals clashing, then flowed effortlessly into a pulse rioting rhumba.

"I beg your pardon?" The waiter's big brown eyes, soft as a cow's, managed to look as helpless. His bald head gleamed in the soft light, the perfectly trimmed fringe of hair above his ears appeared to be holding on grimly to keep from sliding further down that round skull.

"I said I want sauerkraut and wieners," Barby repeated in a loud voice. The people at the next table looked our way.

"*Eh Bien!*" the waiter said softly, showing us his French. "I am but so sorry. We close the dinner serving at eleven o'clock." He not only showed us his French, but his accent proved him French.

"Look, Frenchy," I said patiently. "The lady wants sauerkraut and wieners. Does she get sauerkraut and wieners?" I showed him a five-dollar bill. "This is for the chef, compre?"

"I see," he said doubtfully, plucking the bill from my fingers. He vanished into a set of double doors.

Twenty bucks—and I didn't have a drink yet. I saw visions of myself doing the dishes. Sauerkraut and wieners would probably cost another twenty and if we drank—?

Barby patted my hand.

"I knew you were Beverly Hills class when I saw you at the Boat Club." She put her elbows on the table, twined her fingers together, making a bridge. On the bridge she rested her soft round chin, her lids half-covering those big green eyes. "I just love to spend my time with Beverly Hills class men. My evening time and my morning after time," she said huskily.

I felt the fire starting in my stomach. The heat from it must have got in my eyes. Barby grinned wickedly.

"Down, boy, down," she whispered. "The night's young—but promising."

Mr. Five by Five with the soft brown eyes appeared at the table. It looked like his eyes were going to melt and run down his cheeks.

"The chef, he's Italian," he said sorrowfully. "He not like us French. Non, non." With a reverent look, he laid the fiver gently on the table.

"No sauerkraut and wieners?" Barby asked flatly.

"Sorry." The waiter shrugged his round shoulders. His brown eyes said he was crying for shame with having failed.

"That's that," Barby said lightly. "I'll take a Pink Lady. I'll bet Roscoe Todd just loves Pink Ladies, too." She nodded her head at me.

"Not Pink Ladies in a glass," I said. "And you can call me Toddy—all my friends do. I'll take scotch on the rocks."

"Toddy...." Barby mused, cocked her head to one side. "That wouldn't be a hot toddy, would it?"

"Tonight I'm strictly a hot toddy," I said, letting the heat light my eyes.

"I'll try my best to catch cold," she said teasingly. "So I'll need a hot toddy before morning. A pink lady out of her glass with a hot toddy ought to be fun.

"Let's dance!" She was out of her chair and heading for the dance floor, showing me her swaying hips as she moved between the tables.

Rhumba. Beat of pulse. Surrendering twisting body. Breast to chest. Soft flesh molding. Turning, swaying, heartbeat to drumbeat to undulating torso. In your grasp but out of your reach. Coaxing, tempting, teasing, denying. Dish on the table, but the plate empty. Dying on a downbeat, the feast finished, but the feaster famished.

Back at the table, the scotch took the heat from my head. Barby sipped her Pink Lady, the laughing imps in her eyes telling me she knew to the last inch my raising temperature.

"Care to try your luck?" she asked elfishly.

"Here?" I said, startled.

"Gambling. Upstairs. Silly!" she laughed, tipping her head back. "You get to try that kind of luck on the way home."

I gave it to her straight.

"I haven't got that kind of money," I said. "I don't carry a thousand in loose change with me. I can go fifty, but that's chicken feed here."

"It'll buy you fifty whites. I'll match you fifty so we'll have a hundred. We split fifty-fifty, win, lose, or draw."

She opened the small cosmetic case she carried, took out two tightly folded bills. Peeled them apart, dropped one fifty on the table, put the other back in the case.

"Ransom money," she explained demurely. "So I can always catch a cab home."

I picked up the fifty, dusted the face powder from it. The perfume almost got my thermometer out of control again.

"A hundred dollars wouldn't help a girl like you out of a tight spot." I let my eyes travel slowly and hotly over the swelling breasts, small waist, the white soft flesh between the low neck of the gown. "With what you got, it would take a gun. A big gun, at that. Say a .45 automatic."

She made her green eyes big.

"Now where do you suppose I could hide a big gun?" she asked, her eyes eager and mocking. "And what would I need a gun for? I don't use the money before." She was laughing. "I use it afterwards—after he passes out and I have to go home." She stood up, took both of my hands in hers, pulled me to my feet. "Let's go up and see if Lady Luck is also smiling at you?"

CHAPTER ELEVEN

W E WENT UP THE WIDE CURVING STAIRS at the other end of the ballroom. Plush. Strictly plush. But business. Soft murmur of voices. Cashier's cage just in the door. Any game you wanted. I spotted the troubleshooters, big heavy guys in tuxes, three of them. Their faces were slightly scarred, ears wrinkled from gloves, but quiet, not drinking. Rumor had it they never hit a customer, just one on each side, holding his arms, carrying him so his feet were touching the floor, the third man walking close in front. Casual. Easy. Take him outside, order his car, put him in. If necessary, use a company car, take him home. But never, never create a disturbance. The suckers might quit gambling to look. Bad for business.

I went to the cashier's cage, got a hundred whites. The guy was as happy as if I had a hundred eagles. I turned to Barby.

"What's your disgrace?"

"Say a number," she said.

"Two?"

"Even," she said. "Your choice. If it had been odd, it would have been mine."

"21?"

"My game!" she said excitedly. "I knew we felt alike. I love 21!"

The game room boasted a moderate crowd. The 21 table had a few vacancies. We eased onto stools, gave the dealer a nod. He dropped a card in front of Barby. She rode. King, deuce. Twelve or three. Rode again. Caught a five. Seventeen or eighteen. She stood.

I caught an ace. An eight. Eighteen or nine. I rode. A deuce. Twenty or eleven. Stood.

The dealer rode his to eighteen. Took Barby's money. Paid me.

Some places 21 is called Blackjack, the army for one. I had played it for hours, days at a time. It's fast, so is the time while playing. I forgot Barby. Until I felt her hand on my arm.

"It's two o'clock, Darling," she said. "Want to quit?"

"Sure," I said, my mind off the game instantly. "Ready to go?"

She looked at the table in front of her, grinned ruefully. Three white chips remained.

"Want some of mine?"

"I've had it," she said lightly.

"Okay. Let's go over and tally." I palmed my chips.

We went to the cashier's cage. Not bad. Built my fifty to one-thirty-two. Barby's three made one-thirty-five. Sixty-seven-fifty apiece. She stuffed hers absently into the cosmetic case.

"Might need that case to powder your nose. Have money all over the floor," I said jokingly.

"I'm not going to powder my nose," she said evenly. "It would get rubbed off. How fast can you pay the waiter at the table, get your car and me in it to your apartment?"

"Real fast," I said instantly.

"Then move, Darling," she said on a soft pulsing breath. "And no games on the way in. I couldn't stand it. I'll pay my bet at the apartment...."

I looked into her green eyes. It was there. Naked, unashamed. Free for me to see.

She snuggled up close in the car, took my free hand in both of hers, rubbed it against her face, kissed the fingers lightly.

The 'Bird lost a lot of rubber in the run to Saratoga Street. I helped her from the car. She walked lightly, dreamily, in a still, quiet pulsing muse. She waited patiently while I opened the door. I slipped my arm around her waist as we walked down the short hall. I snapped on the soft red light over the studio couch.

Barby swung her body against mine. Her fingers dug into my shoulders. She strained to me. Her eyes were hot, demanding, wanting.

"Now, darling. Now!" she said on a choking breath.

I sat utterly relaxed on the sofa across the room from Barby. She was stretched full length on the couch, her hands folded flatly over her navel, eyes closed. I watched her breasts raise and fall with her quietened breathing. The soft red light turned her white flesh into a dusty orange glow, highlighting the valleys and touching the mountain tops with pink.

I was trying to make up my mind. I wanted a cigaret bad. But was Barby really sleeping, or just relaxing? If I lighted a cigaret and she saw my face, she might leave the apartment without bothering to dress. I didn't want that.

On the other hand, a cigaret would taste nice. Almost as nice as the cherry lipstick smeared on my mouth. The cherry lipstick on my mouth was a satisfying touch. It meant that we had kissed, among other things. And that she hadn't noticed that my lips were made of plastic, with skin over it. My future looked far brighter.

Maybe the docs at the Naval hospital rode the thing too hard, had made me too self-conscious. I decided to try a good long kiss when Barby wasn't too emotional, then watch her reaction. It would be nice to pet normally, friendly like, with a girl again. But knowing that under the proper emotional pressure I could do a little necking without scaring the girl to death was a help. A big help.

I decided against the smoke, better to wait a few minutes and then go over and sit beside Barby. I was glad I decided to wait.

"I bet you think I'm common," Barby said, opening her eyes and turning her face to me. "I mean the way I rushed you out of Beverly Hills and up to this apartment."

Her comment took me back years. Seems as if every girl asks the same things afterwards. The reply can ruin all the fun if you're not careful. I liked the fun.

"On the contrary," I said seriously. "I think you are very uncommon. An adult, both emotionally and physically. A beautiful, mature, living doll. Not afraid of giving, of sharing a wonderful feeling, or dropping convention when wanting or sharing a bed. If all girls were like you, this would be a wonderful world. I adore you and your emotions," I ended softly.

"You come here," she said huskily. "I like my men close when they're making love to me." She shifted her tantalizing body over, making room for me to sit beside her. I sat beside her.

She placed both my hands in a very nice position, ran her fingers up my arms onto my shoulder.

"Now say that again," she whispered hungrily. I said it again. She smiled dreamily.

"You know," she said softly, "I sat watching you play 21. I watched your profile, the way you used your fingers, the stillness of your face, with only the eyes really alive, and I became fascinated. I could feel my flesh tingling, the blood start pounding. I thought this is how he felt when he danced with me. This is how he feels when he looks at me, with the heat in his eyes. He's not ashamed, why should I be?

"The longer I watched you, the more bothered I got. I even forgot I was playing 21. But you never noticed." She smiled slightly. "I was almost afraid to disturb you, but I was still more afraid not to. If I had watched you much longer, I don't know if my knees would have held me up when I tried to stand. The longer I watched you, the more I wanted you," she finished huskily. Her pink tongue moistened her lips, slipped back in, leaving the lips softly shining and open. Back in her eyes a fire was burning brightly.

Now's the time, I thought inanely, see if she notices your lips when you kiss her, before she gets too far gone.

I leaned slowly forward, set my mouth to hers, twisted slightly against her burning lips. That was as far as my thinking got. Emotion took over with a consuming blaze.

Hours and centuries later she pushed me gently by the shoulder, ran her hand through my curly hair.

"I'd like a cigaret," she said in that special voice of lovers.

I went to the end table, kept my back to her, lighted the cigaret, took a long satisfying drag. When I gave it to her, she placed it between her parted lips. She inhaled luxuriously, sat up.

"I'd better be going," she said sadly. "I'll bet its almost morning."

I glanced at the window. The sky was already light in the east.

"No hurry," I said, and meant it. "I have a double bed and all the makings for a late breakfast."

She wrinkled her nose at me, stood up and stretched.

"Don't do that, Honey," I warned. "Or the next time you ask for a cigaret it will be noon."

She laughed gaily, did a few suggestive dance steps, dodged my reaching hand.

"I'd love to stay," she said seriously. "But I can't. Another time, another night, and...." She left the promise hang in the air meaningfully.

"No. Please," she said as I reached for my clothes. "I'll call a cab." She picked up the phone, dialed, her eyes laughing at me. "It'll take you ten minutes to dress. I can be dressed and home

CREATURE OF SIN

by that time. Besides, you might sell me on the idea of parking somewhere for awhile."

She asked for my address, ordered the cab. She picked up the pad by the phone, wrote something, tore the paper off, laid it by the phone.

"Your number, Lover-boy?" she asked.

"You got it," I answered promptly.

"Your phone number. Silly!"

She wrote it down as I gave it to her, tore the sheet loose from the pad, walked over and put it in her compact.

"Thanks for the number," she said, wriggling into her dress. "Left you mine." As her head burst from the top of the dress she said seriously. "And I want you to use it Please?"

"That's a promise. I'll wear it out. The phone company will make you install an extra one so that they can break even on the service."

"I'd gladly pay the extra charge," she said, twisting her feet into her slippers, picking up her cosmetic case. She tossed her coppery hair back, patted it into place. Opened her cosmetic case, straightened her lipstick. A car horn blew.

"My cab," Barby said, glanced hurriedly around, decided she forgot nothing. I caught her at the door. She turned, kissed me lightly on the lips.

"Thanks for a wonderful evening," she said through the closing door. I heard the cab door slam, the motor throb heavily and die away.

CHAPTER TWELVE

WALKED SLOWLY BACK INTO THE LIVING ROOM, noticing that the early dawn was lighting the room. I clicked off the red light over the couch. I felt let down, but more alive than I had since '45. I walked restlessly around the apartment, lighted a cigaret. This night had marked a change in my thinking, in my living.

I had spent almost an entire night in the company of a witty, vivacious girl, trading talk, bantering, trading love, living. No where during the night had I slipped, at no time had my facial muscles demanded that I smile or laugh. The impulse had only gone to my eyes. My sub-conscious had finally taken control, like a man that habitually reaches for an earlobe, not knowing he's doing it; like a dreamer eating, not knowing he's doing it, not tasting the food. Now my laugh, my frown, my smile, would habitually go to my eyes, not to my face muscles. I had taken one long step back to entering society.

But I had something to do, a score to even. I was in deep, even if I wanted to quit. A matter of time, until Mule and his partner were told to frame me, to go to the police as eyewitnesses to Sheila's murder.

It was a threat hanging over me. If all other methods failed, that was the boss's trump card, the ace card up his murdering sleeve. I looked at the clock. Five-thirty.

I had to be in court at nine. Monday morning at nine, the desk sergeant had said, as the clerk had taken my two hundred dollars bail. I decided that two hours of sleep was a chance I couldn't afford to take. Two hundred dollars worth of chance.

I went into the bathroom, climbed into the tub, pulled the curtains, let the cold shower needle me. As I went into the living-room, I picked up my suit, emptied the pockets, and decided it needed the cleaners.

Dressed in light tan slacks, dark tan ribbed weave sportscoat over a tieless white silk summer shirt, I counted my money, decided I had better drop by the bank, then remembered the two hundred bail money. Going into the kitchen, I was suddenly rav-enously hungry, so I peeled off my sportscoat.

Two thick slices of ham, six eggs and three cups of coffee later I felt wonderful—and sleepy. I looked at my wristwatch. Seven o'clock. Two hours to go. I could go down to my office, maybe find another letter in my mail slot.

I left the apartment. The early morning air was soft and warm, heavy with moisture. On the coast it would mean rain. Here in Newport it meant only another hot, muggy day. But that would come later. I looked at the 'Bird. Almost imagined I could see Barby sitting in it, then decided to walk.

The streets were waking up. Monday morning. Back to work. The daily grind. Something I didn't have to worry about, not for a long time. What with almost three hundred dollars a month pension coming in.

At least coming in until I had adjusted, got myself in a position where I could earn my own way. The Naval Board had insisted on it. They didn't want me having to work with people. As the Colonel had said, if I started to laugh in some office, it might mean a riot. Besides, I made people uncomfortable. The brooding stillness of my face worked on them, if they had to be around me too much.

I let myself laugh, there on the street, knowing that the laugh was in my eyes only, because the thought of Barby and last night had suddenly got tangled up with what the Colonel had said about people having to be around me too much. She was certainly around me, around me and all over me.

I cut across to Momouth Street, down Momouth to Fourth, over Fourth to York. On the corner I went into the office building and up the steps to my office. I opened the door, looked in the mail slot, found an envelope. I glanced at the left hand corner ... my bank.

I went through the small empty reception room, opened the door to my inner office, sat down behind the desk and opened the letter.

My bank statement, with cancelled checks. Over eight thousand dollars worth, but the balance was still hefty, thirty-six thousand, eight hundred, twenty dollars and sixty one cents. The money I had no use for from '42 to '58.

Take sixteen years of a man's life and hand him a little over forty thousand dollars, plus enough to live on every month. I tried to feel bitter, was surprised to find that I couldn't. Before it had been easy. All I had to do was think of yesterday and taste the gall in my mouth. But not today.

Funny what a woman and her giving can do to you. I decided not to try and rationalize that. Much too deep. The effect was the interesting thing. Very interesting.

I glared at my bank balance again, trying to feel the old bitterness. Gone. Instead I felt good. All the good things it could buy. But it couldn't buy Kirk back....

I sat looking at the desk, seeing Kirk. His easy laughing nature, his full of life healthy body ... His way of squeezing my arm when the going got rough ... The thrill of the two of us against the world at fifteen ... A long time ago, with the years crowding in between … Useless, bitter years. The cry for help in the plain white envelope.… why hadn't I answered it?

Did the Navy docs have me? Or did I have me? Did my feeling sorry for myself, my hating myself, my being afraid of myself, do that to Kirk?

I could have gone, but I was afraid of the look of loathing on strangers' faces when they saw me—of being shunned by a society that wouldn't understand. And Kirk, what would he have done when he saw me? Probably dropped everything here, taken me back, stood beside me, did his best to help. Probably, hell, he would have.

So I had let him down. Twice. Once by not asking for his help. The second time by not answering his plea for help. It was damnable of me for not confiding in him when I wrote, for playing my condition light, for bragging of the easy thing I had of it at the hospital. Minor skin condition, I wrote him, taking the docs for a ride. Living like a king, the few times I did write. For Kirk was always on the move, and until I got a letter from him, I didn't know where to write.

Too late now. Too late for Kirk. But not too late for his killer. No, the killer was on vacation—on vacation from stoking the fires of hell.

And Sheila—Big John spoke the truth last night. He was in no condition to think of lying. Not with that drug tearing his guts up, my shoe grinding his face in the ground. Sheila had said that Big John had tricked her into going for bed money. Big John had said that he would kill anyone he caught messing with her.

So Sheila was in some trouble that Big John didn't know about—or she was a trap. A sexy desirable trap. But she didn't know that she would end up as dead bait. She had made the trap as nice as she could for me—if it was a trap.

So I owed her something. Under other circumstances, just ten dollars, or whatever the going rate was. But now—well, now she rated second to Kirk.

Something could be worth only ten dollars in a bed, but suddenly, under other circumstances, in the sand it could be worth life. Hers—and mine, if I didn't work fast enough. The killers, if I could. I looked at my wristwatch. Eight twenty.

I stood up, went out, locking the office behind me. Taking my time, I wasn't hiring a lawyer. I would plead guilty to disturbing the peace. I wondered idly if Big John would be there. I wanted him there. I wanted to watch him, watch him like a snake watching a bird. Let him know that I wasn't finished with him yet. No, not yet. I wanted to use his greasy carcass as a crowbar, to pry the gang apart with, if I could.

I walked up the steps to the courthouse lawn, hearing the birds chirping in the trees, feeling the warm softness in the morning air.

The case moved fast. The judge was bored and apparently suffering from a hangover. I pleaded guilty to disturbing the peace, the lawyer for Big John and his pals pleaded guilty to everything, paid their fine, the judge, with bored indifference, dropped the assault to kill charge.

Big John was waiting with his group outside the court-room as I came out after paying the twenty-five dollar fine. His lawyer hurried over to me.

"I am Lawrence Jerkins," he said, sticking out a thin bony hand. I ignored it. He wrapped his hand about his briefcase carefully, but held the smooth smile on his face. "My client wishes you to know that he appreciates your not telling the court the circumstances. Of course, I am prepared to repay you—whatever the amount is—for the inconvenience this has caused you."

I walked over to Big John, the lawyer watching me uneasily. I stopped in front of the discolored face.

"You oily pig—," I said carefully, "—I did you no favors this morning. You owe me nothing. You know that what we have to settle has nothing to do with the law, not the kind of law we have in courtrooms." Big John kept his eyes averted, but the color was creeping up his neck. But the color of anger working up his neck couldn't wipe the sheen of fear showing in his eyes.

"It's your kind of law I'm using against you and your kind," I continued coldly. "Jungle law. We held court with jungle law last night. That was a small potatoes court. Like this court was here today. Wait until I get my big case, gutter rat. A real big case—where I will be the judge and jury and the executioner.

"I'm building that case fast, tell your boss that. Tell the boss time is running out."

I turned on my heel, bumping into an owlish looking man wearing spectacles. He had a notebook and pencil out, making pothooks rapidly. I heard Big John curse under his breath. I kept coming around on my heel in time to see Big John grab the owlish looking man's notebook. The man made a feeble effort to snatch it back. Big John ruthlessly dug him in the gut with his elbow.

"Mr. Macotta! Please!" Jerkins said sharply. "No trouble in the courthouse. Don't step too far out of line.… some things lawyers can't take care of." Jerkins alarm was real. The allusion he made was not about the law.

"Can't let these little squirts start making trouble," Big John rasped. "You know the orders on that."

"I like trouble!" I snapped, fastening my right hand over his knuckles. I braced and put on the pressure. Big John's lips twitched as he winced.

"Drop it," I whispered softly. "Drop it or I'll break your wrist!" I raised my free hand in the start of a savage chop to the thick wrist peeping out from under the starched shirt-cuff.

Big John dropped the notebook. The man with the spectacles swooped, grabbed it.

"Thanks," he said and disappeared in the crowd.

I let Big John's knuckles loose. He shook his hand and flexed it.

"Want to try throwing it, punk Go ahead, throw that hand at my face—I'd like nothing better than to make a spoon fed bottle baby out of you."

I waited, taunting him with the derision in my eyes.

"Now just a minute—," Jerkins babbled frantically, "—let's not have any trouble...."

"Trouble," I snorted. "You got trouble, you little two-bit weasel. Get out of my way before you get squashed—get out of this town before you end up on a marble slab." I elbowed him aside, headed for the door and some fresh air. Almost jarred the heavy door from its hinges as I straight-armed it open.

"Regular bull in a china shop, ain't'cha?" Hogarth said caustically. "Got a minute?"

"Had your say with the judge, didn't you?" I snapped.

He shrugged. "All in a day's work," he said easily. "Thought you should know who the man with the horn-rimmed glasses represents." He jerked his hand in the direction of the court-house lawn. "He's waiting on one of those benches to have a word with you. He's a top reporter from one of the big dailies."

"So?"

"So you had better not shoot off your mouth to him like you did to me."

"Why not? No skin off my nose. Might help some to let the public know under one headline about the ugliness of Newport's crime. How it follows a pattern."

"Put the public on my neck, Todd, and so help me, I'll put you in jail and keep you there," he bit it off savagely.

"You have to have charges."

"Charges! I can get enough from last night at the Barby to keep you in jail for a year. Don't think that waitress won't finger you if I put the heat on her! But I'm giving you the benefit of the doubt. I'm not looking for something to book you on," he said grudgingly, looking at me from under his thick brows. "Maybe you're right. Maybe I'm drawing my salary and coasting. You can think what you like. But I'm keeping book—make one bad move and I'll hit you with it."

"He wasn't making those pothooks for nothing," I said testily. "So what'll I tell him? Only make it worse to hem and haw."

I knew Hogarth meant it when he said that he would keep his hands off. I also knew it cost him a lot in pride to tell me so. He was the only friendly acquaintance I had. I'd like to keep it that way as long as I could.

"What you tell him is your problem." He turned to the double doors, paused. "I've always given them a lot of general information, but nothing definite until I had it. I don't think you have anything definite yet?"

If he only knew, I thought, how much I had that was definite! The loaded dice, the note from Sheila, the murder at Tacoma, the ape from Chicago. Four definites—with one that could put me away for life, with the others assorted jail terms.

"Nothing definite yet," I assured him.

Horn-rimmed spectacles came off the bench like a Springer Spaniel as I strode toward him. He had a long body with short arms and legs, brown hair that fingers had traveled in a lot, brown eyes, a long nose that was rounded at the nostrils, thin lips and shoved back chin. A Springer Spaniel with glasses, I thought glumly, you can't shake a Spaniel from a trail, cold or hot.

"Mr. Todd?" Springer Spaniel said. He held a card between his index fingers. I took it. Press card. Horace Matthews.

"What can I do for you, Mr. Matthews?" I asked, handing him back his press card. He looked at me shrewdly. I could swear I saw the end of that long nose twitch.

"Three questions: what was the fight about Saturday night; what was the fight about Sunday night—and what are you trying to do besides get yourself killed?" The words came out in a staccato burst.

"If I'm going to answer all three, we'd better sit down, don't you think?"

"Right." He collapsed back on the bench, notebook and pencil appearing in his fingers.

"I'm going to tell you—but under one condition," I said flatly.

"Money?"

"Not money. I'm going to give you the whole story, but you can't use it yet—not all of it."

"Why?"

"Because it doesn't have an ending—not yet. Anything that I tell you now I'll deny if questioned, so let's just say that I'll spin you a yarn, like I was talking about some character that was wandering around town. Not a word of truth to it, you understand?"

"And when do I get the truth?" he asked. "When will the fairy godmother wave the magic wand that will turn fantasy into fact?"

"If I live to the end of the story, the police will confirm," I said quietly. "Else my death notice will have to do."

"Hmmmm." He worried the pencil with his teeth, then raked the pencil absently through his tousled hair. He looked into my eyes, his nose twitched slightly. I actually saw it twitch. He suddenly shot out one bony hand.

"Bargain," he said. "Let's have it."

I gave it to him—all of it. In the third person, about a guy named Screwball.

"Hot," he said when I finished. "Hot as hell. Hard to hold. You'll read something in the next edition. You'll have a thousand people calling you if I use your name. I won't. They'll smell you—I mean Screwball—out anyway. Be ready. Luck." He shot his bony hand out again, wrung mine. "Need help, holler."

"Thanks," I said dryly,"—but the kind of help I need you fellows don't believe in."

"No?" he paused in the act of starting to gallop away.

"You know the name of a good fortune teller?" I asked wryly. "A look in her crystal ball might help."

"Not joking," he barked. "You said muscle is what the organization uses. You're fighting with muscle. I can line up two ton of muscle. Do what you want, no questions asked."

I thought that over. "Muscle boys running wild in Newport. Street corner fights. Barroom fights. Newport taking on the rough and tumble action of a frontier town in the gold rush days of the forty niners. No, it wouldn't work. Everything would go under cover. Mean a couple more months of waiting for the rats to crawl out of their holes. But I'll keep it in mind."

"Yeah, probably would," he said over his shoulder as he galloped off.

The hot morning sun beat down on my shoulders, made its heat felt through my sportcoat. I headed for my office. The hands on my wristwatch were squeezing the morning to a close. Eleven ten. I was starting to feel the effects of no sleep for a day and a night. There would be nothing doing at the office, be a good place to catch a few winks.

The office was cool, with the coolness of unused places. I didn't want to open a window and leave the hot muggy air in. I sat on a chair, folded my arms on the desk and dropped my head on them.

My thoughts drifted idly. I got a hold on Big John, went to jail, got to Sheila, she got killed. Got Big John again, found out the name of the man who had probably killed Sheila—and Kirk. Got a reporter interested—might get some publicity. Banged up one of their imported muscle boys. Next step—Mule. After that, if I wasn't in jail, start banging the tin horns around on general principles, put the pressure on, see who would crack first, the boss—or me.

I came suddenly awake, the insistent clamor of the telephone shrill in the still room. I reached over and took the handpiece from the cradle.

"Hello," I said drowsily. "Todd speaking."

"Matthews," came the bark. "Thought awhile. Talked to Sergeant Hogarth. He seems to think you haven't got your marbles. Said something about a Naval doctor. Didn't tell Hogarth a thing."

"Okay," I said. "Why bother me again?"

"Want to check you with the Naval Hospital." His staccato voice barked on the wire. "Mind?"

"Why?"

"Could get into a lot of trouble. Big Paper. Libel suits cost money, even when facts are only inferred."

"Call this number." I gave him the hospital number. "Ask for Doctor Slyneadi—that's pronounced slide and die. He'll give you the dope. Might tell him that the assault charge was dropped. Save me calling him."

"Good." The wire sang with emptiness. I thought maybe he had hung up. "If what you say is true, you have a big bite to swallow," he barked suddenly. "Sure you can swing it?"

"I can try," I said quietly.

"Hate to twist your arm," he shot back. "I'd like to detail a couple of strong arm boys to side you."

"Thanks again," I said patiently. "While you're talking to the doc, ask about my condition. You know that a blind man develops an uncanny sense of feel? A legless man develops huge arm, chest and shoulder muscles? Nature's way of compensating. Nature took away my flesh; she poured the unused energy back into my muscles. A few bullets, a baseball bat or knife might stop me. Bare hands won't. The reason why this racket has gone on so long is because they depend on bare hands for weapons."

"A fight.... who knows who started it," he barked back. "Broken neck. In a wreck or fall.... I can understand it. Even if proved the man was killed in a fistfight, the most is involuntary manslaughter. Out in a year. Damned clever. I'm checking. If okay, with you all the way. Bye for now." I heard the phone go on the hook.

I thought of cradling my head on my arms again. Looked at my watch ... Been sleeping three hours ... After two ... Would feel better if I wrapped myself around a big steak. I got up, had the doorknob in my hand. The telephone shrilled. Probably Matthews calling back. I lifted the receiver.

"Roscoe Todd?" The voice was metallic, flat, dead.

"Yes," I said, instantly alert.

"I'm offering you a job," the metallic voice droned. "Good pay, easy hours. Make as much as you want Ten thousand dollar stake to start."

It had come. The boss was on the other end of the wire. I felt every nerve tingling.

"In the bank?" I asked softly. I was trying to place the metallic sound. Didn't have the blur of a tape recorder....

"So you know about the joint accounts." It was a statement. "That won't help you."

"Why do you want me on the team?"

"You're strong. You're ruthless. You know how to gamble," the metallic voice purred. "You are a lot of trouble. I want the trouble on my side, keeping my business in line."

"And if I decide that I want you more than I want your filthy money?"

"Then you don't have long to live. Your freedom is even shorter. You make the choice now." The metallic device the person was using made the words sound even deadlier.

"Where can I see you?" A slim chance, but I knew the answer before I asked.

"You can't. Ever. This is my way of contact Try and find me, you die. Your choice?"

CHAPTER THIRTEEN

"PLAY YOUR HAND!" I snapped at the boss's hard voice. "Make sure you have all trumps. Make one wrong play and you are cold meat. Remember one thing: I'm playing your way. Cards up my sleeve, muscle to muscle, mayhem for mayhem. I'll get to you if I have to break every bone in every muscleman you can hire. I'm going to find the crack in your armor and when I find that crack, I'll rip it off that filthy body of yours and crush you with my hands, bit by filthy bit." The chill rage in my voice had the hair at the nape of my neck trying to stand up. The person who had ordered Kirk's murder—bargaining with me! "You murdering fiend! I wouldn't bargain with you if you were the devil himself and we were in hell burning each other with flame throwers!"

"That's final?" the deadly metallic voice asked.

"Damned final—as final as the ace of spades."

"I'll put the ace of spades on your casket." The wire went dead.

I beat on the button to get the operator. Ages later the calm voice of the operator came on the wire.

"I want the number of the party who just called. It's urgent."

"Sorry. We can't trace a dial call."

"You can. In this case, you had better. The party threatened my life. Or should I get the police to check?" An idle threat, but a gamble.

"Just a minute, please."

I waited, hoping. I needn't have.

"Sorry. That was an unlisted phone. We cannot give the number," she said, with the meaning clear. Phone operators are aware of all the tricks used to get the unlisted number of classified telephones.

I put the receiver back on the cradle. Still no closer to the boss. The big guy. But I had him worried, bothered enough to call me, to offer a job. But now the deck was cut, the game was on. I had to gamble on bluffing the dealer to hell. But one play I couldn't bluff, and I was afraid of that one.

Frame me for Sheila. It made me cold to think of it. My only chance was to crowd him, to play fast and furious, to rip and tear the cards, to upset the table, force him to make one bad play—or her. I still felt that it wasn't a man in back of the gambling ring.

I got up from the desk. I still needed that steak. After the steak, I could go to the apartment, get some shut eye. While I had the time. If things started happening, I might not get to sleep. For a long time. Or maybe I would get plenty. Forever.

I dawdled over my meal, let myself relax. I thought of Barby, of last night. Letting the pleasure pour through my body at the memory, I almost decided to go to the apartment and call her. But if I talked to her, I would want to see her. I knew it. I had other things to do tonight ... important things.

I had to find where Mule was holed up. Big John would help me on that. He would have to. It meant going back in the Barby again. So what? Maybe another riot. If they wanted to play rough, could I help it?

I paid my bill. As I walked out, a paper boy was stuffing the late edition in one of those bags that hang on a telephone pole. I stuck my seven cents in the slot, pulled out a paper. I had no idea if anything would be in this paper, tomorrow's paper or the day after. I did know that three big dailies in one tri-city area make for competition, and competition telescopes time. If my reporter was a big enough name.... he was.

Bold type. Down in the left-hand corner of the front page. Slick. No names. The account of the court hearing, the hint that gambling was the cause. That the defendant was questioned by the judge. That said defendant was a counselor, interested in collecting money that innocent people lost to crooked gamblers, with a strong hint that more was to come. That the lid was going to lift, letting the stink out. Nothing definite, but enough could be read between the lines.

The boss was going to have to move now—fast. I had cut the safety margin by opening my mouth to the newspaper. I could sense the danger drawing close. Rereading the article, I knew the ace of spades had been dealt, that it was lying blind on the poker table. It was time I dealt at least one ace of spades from my sleeve—time that Mule drew his first.

I dropped the paper in a trash can. No going to the apartment now for some shut-eye. Find Big John. It was early, but I had to chance it. Someone at the Barby would know his address. Might take a few broken bones to get it, but I'd get it. I headed for my apartment, but only to pick up the 'Bird parked there.

The Barby had a few working stiffs sitting at the bar. Steel chips in their hair, iron dust ground into their hands ... From the local machine shops ... Drinking a quiet beer before going home. I hooked my arm on the rail, ordered a scotch.

The barkeep set the shot glass in front of me, reached back and got the bottle of White Horse, then looked into my face. Recognition came quickly, but he didn't slop the drink.

"Looking for Big John," I said.

"Thought so," he grunted, taking my money.

"He's here?"

"No." The barkeep set the bottle back, looked at me. "Glad he ain't."

"Save you a lot of trouble if you told me where to find him," I said evenly.

"Don't doubt that," he said shortly.

"Then give."

"Me?"

"You."

"I'm not his daddy," the barkeep rasped.

I looked at him. Steadily. He wiped the bar nervously with his rag, waited on one of the steel-chips-in-hair boys.

"I don't want no trouble," he said finally.

I didn't answer that.

"If you called this number, he might answer." He dropped a card on the bar. I ignored it

"I'll wait for him here," I said dryly. He caught on.

"The cops again, huh?"

"If he's not a nice boy—yes."

"Him—a nice boy?" He snorted. "Hell, it's no skin off my nose. Go wreck his apartment this time." He turned the card over, went down the bar to wipe some dampness off. I read the address, downed my scotch, went out the door and gunned the 'Bird.

Big John holed up on Eleventh. Lot of big apartments there. I found the number, went up the steps to the second floor. His apartment number on the door has done in faded and chipped goldplate. I tried the knob. The door came open. Sure of himself, the big tin horn, I thought, not even bothering to lock his door. I stepped in.

Three of them were there, Big John, Tim and Jackson, sitting at the table in shirt-sleeves, an open whiskey bottle keeping them company. Big John's damaged ear was on my side as he swung his head to look at me. All three froze, sat watching me.

"Hi," I said. "Just a friendly visit. Want to know where Mule is holed up."

"Damn you," Big John blustered.

"What about you other mugs? Wanta talk?" I asked.

"Go to hell," Tim said.

"Up your a-hole," Jackson sneered.

"You're not being polite. I might get mad," I warned. Tim and Jackson shoved their chairs back from the table. I picked an empty chair up, setting by the door.

I turned it bottom side up, ripped a leg loose, dropped the broken chair. Slowly I took the wooden leg at each end, broke it in two. The popping and splintering grated on their nerves. I held the broken ends up, showing the raw, splintery edges.

"These wouldn't feel nice," I said, "grinding around in your faces."

Tim licked his suddenly dry lips. Jackson looked at Big John.

"No hurry," I said quietly. "But I'm getting impatient."

"Whatta you want with Mule?" Big John tried to growl, but wheezed instead.

"I want to play patta cake," I said dryly. "Maybe like he did with your girl friend."

Big John's face went gray. Tim and Jackson looked at him questioningly. Evidently he hadn't told them of my recent conversation with him, the one where I had my heel in his ear.

"Whatta'ya mean?" he rasped uneasily.

"Maybe your two pals would like to know about our little talk last night. Or would you rather tell me where I can find Mule." I waved the broken chair leg. "Don't want to use these right now. Later on I might love to. In about two seconds later on. Where do I find Mule?"

They looked at each other. It was plain each was afraid to talk in front of the other. The great common fear of the unknown boss locked their lips. That was all right. My job was to make them more afraid of someone else. They lived by fear, so they answered to the greatest fear. Logical.

"Tell you what," I said coldly. "You're afraid to talk in front of each other. I can fix that. I'll brain two of you, then the one left can tell me."

I moved. Tim was closest. All three started a mad scramble to get their feet under them. I smacked Tim over the head with the broken chairleg. As he slumped back into his chair, I put the splintered end of the leg into his face, shoved him and the chair crashing across the room into the wall.

Big John and Jackson collapsed back onto their chairs. Big John started shaking, his free hand pulling at the fingers sticking out of the cast on his right arm. Jackson stared fascinated at Tim's bloody face under the chair by the wall.

"One more to go," I said savagely. I banged both ends of the broken leg onto the table. "I'm talking your language, punks. Split skull for split skull. Where does Mule hole up?"

"He's over on Keturah Street," Big John said sullenly. "Not that it'll do you any good. He'll break you in half."

"The number, tin horn," I snapped.

"Forty-three," he said. "I hope to hell he tears your guts out."

"You keep right on hoping, you two bit bastard. But don't bank on it. You two take that punk and pack your clothes. Get out! I'm declaring open house on your kind, beginning now. The next time I see any of you, I'm not going to talk. I'm going to bust you all over the landscape." The brutality these men represented twisted my guts, made me cringe at wallowing in the same bloodlust with them, made me hate myself at the sudden thrill that poured through me when I heard their bones cracking. The self hate died suddenly when I remembered Kirk—and Sheila.

"You been dishing this stuff out for years," I said savagely. I smashed one of the broken chair legs down on Jackson's knuckles lying on the table top. The splintering bone made a beautiful sound. He upset the chair as he threw himself backward, half fell across the floor, sat crouched against the wall, holding his broken hand.

"Too damn many years! I'll crush you quicker than I'd crush a cockroach crawling on the floor. Your boss called me up today, said he was going to fix my clock. So I got nothing to lose by breaking your necks, you stinking bastards. Now get the hell out of town, and get quick, or the explosion will rip your blood sucking bellies open." I threw the broken chair legs in Big John's face. "And if you make a phone call to Mule before I get there, you won't live to get out of town!"

I slammed the door in back of me, on Big John pawing the blood running down his face. I took the steps two at a time, almost running until I hit the seat of the 'Bird and gunned it cruelly away from the curb. Fire was pouring through my veins, the urge to destroy had my stomach in a hard knot. The boss might get to me, but he would get to me alone. Because I was going to get every gorilla I knew, I was going to get them now.

CHAPTER FOURTEEN

KETURAH IS A SHORT STREET, two blocks long, residential. Forty-three looked the same as the rest. I pulled the 'Bird past it, jammed into the curb, got out before the motor quit turning over.

Number 43 was a two-story frame, badly in need of paint. It didn't look like an apartment building. An iron gate wired to a sagging fence barred it from the street. I went between two new cars parked in front, one a Cadillac. Way out of keeping for this neighborhood. Parking a Cadillac on a street like this should have aroused the police's curiosity. To hell with the police. Before this night was over, they would be looking for me. Maybe with a high-powered rifle. I had a feeling that it didn't matter what I did, that within twenty-four hours they would be looking for me with that high-powered rifle anyway.

The hot sun was trying to drown itself behind the hills as I went through the sagging gate, onto the unpainted front porch. Tried the door. Locked. I twisted the knob as far as it would go, put my shoulder to the door. The lock wasn't much good. No one in the front room, hardly any furniture. I scraped a finger over a coffee table. Dust. Maybe Big John had given me a bum steer. I felt the rage come up in my throat at the thought. Then muted voices came to me. I opened the door from the front room. The voices were louder. I walked softly across a small hallway, with steps leading upstairs on one end. Put my hand on the knob of the door in front of me. I could hear voices plainly now.

"See you. And five," someone said.

"Cost you another ten."

"Make it twenty."

I twisted the doorknob, shoved. It wasn't locked. I stepped in, closed the door and leaned back against it.

Five men were sitting at a big old-fashioned round table, the kind you see in family dining rooms. Cards and money were on the table. In the far corner a small man sat on a chair, leaning back, his ankles hooked around the legs, chair-back tilted against the wall. One of the men looked up from the card table, looked back at his cards. The small man on the tilted chair eyed me sharply. I walked swiftly across the room, opened the door into the next room.

It used to be a kitchen. The gas range had a black coffee pot setting on a burner. A wooden table held a whiskey bottle and a melted bowl of ice. Cockroaches were running around the sink. A wooden kitchen cabinet stood astraddle one corner, its doors hanging open, the glass broken out. An army cot was against the wall on my left as I opened the door.

"Hi," the girl said, not trying to cover her naked body stretched full-length on the army cot. "I could use a fiver if you're winning."

I stepped back and pulled the door closed. Sheila Thomson wasn't lying. Not all the way. That was what she had meant by bouncing the bed. That was why prostitution was taboo in Newport. Come to a gambling house and get it free.

I looked at the big hulking blond sitting at the table. He didn't have his black and white checked sportscoat on, but the middle finger on his left hand was neatly bandaged. It was a huge, thick, wide hand, fastened to a bulging arm by a thick hairy wrist. His shirt was open at the throat, showing blond, matted hair. A shovel chin hung over his adam's apple, wide thin-lipped mouth under a button nose. He had pale grey eyes, so pale they looked white under his bushy eyebrows. Those eyes were looking at me, not blinking.

The little man came to his feet, the chair dropping back on all four legs. The men at the table stopped playing, looked questioningly at the blond giant, followed his blank stare to me.

"Hello, Mule," I said softly. "Tell the innocents here the game is over."

"What the hell!" one of the men said, scrambling to his feet.

"It's not a raid?" asked another, undecided. But he got to his feet with a third man.

The three of them grabbed their money on the table, reached for their coats hung over the back of their chairs.

"Hold it!" the little man said silkly. "This is no cop. Just a jerk that don't belong."

His hand made a darting move. A flicker of light winked, sparkled, as he passed the shining blade from hand to hand, faster than the eye could follow. He went into a crouch, his head shoved forward, eyes as blank as a snake's.

"The boss decide muscle was not enough?" I asked tauntingly. "Had to bring in one of the knife monkeys. Looks like you learned your trade south of the border. You kill me with that thing and the police might ask questions." I fought hard at the cold, hard knot of killing rage that was taking hold of me. "Put it away, you damn fool, before I tear you apart!" I said hoarsely. The rage was coming into my face. I could feel the plastic starting to move, as it contorted my features.

The blade faltered in its blinding flicker, picked the rhythm up again. He flattened his lips against his teeth in a snarling grin, showing his small white teeth.

"You going to leave quiet—or do I start cutting your ears off?" he hissed between his locked teeth, his voice quivering with the panic building up in his gut.

Mistakes count. He should have thrown the knife, not taken time to talk. I used the fraction of time to grab a coat from one of the innocents.

I pushed the coat up in front of me, holding it by the shoulders, my eyes peeping over the top. It covered my vitals, down to the waist. His target was my forehead, if he could hit it before I jerked the coat up.

"Throw it, damn you!" I whispered. "Make the one try count. If you miss, you'll never throw another!"

"Let's get the hell out of here!" One of the innocents yelled. I heard them bolt for the door, heard the door slam, then I concentrated on watching that twinkling blade as I started stalking its user.

Mule and the other man remained sitting at the table. I saw Mule lay a huge hand on the arm of the other man as he started to get to his feet.

"Let Blinky have his fun," I heard Mule say in a thin voice. "You try and help him you might get in the way of his knife. We can stomp the bastard after Blinky carves him up."

Blinky was ten feet away. Five. He gave ground. A flicker of fear showed in his opaque eyes. When a knifer flashes a blade, he expects his opponent to flinch, to take water, maybe to run. His opponent walking in on him scares him, takes the advantage of fear away. But a knifer is always dangerous, until you take his knife in your hand or your belly.

Four feet. Three. Blinky's back was against the wall. One more step and he wouldn't have room to throw. The flicker of light changed. I jerked the coat high, felt the blade tug at it, felt a fine burn on my forehead at the hairline. I dropped the coat, grabbed the hand arcing for the back of his neck, going for his hideout blade.

I felt his soft tender hand sock into mine and I crushed the tapering fingers, whipping the hand outward, away from the body, in the direction a hand isn't supposed to go. I snapped down, hearing the wrist crack as it bent back on itself. I poured all my savage strength into that hand, squeezed until I felt the knuckles snap like rotten wood. I slapped his scream back down his throat with my free hand, grabbed his other clawing hand, wrung it like wringing a dishrag, until it was soft and pulpy. Then I kicked him. I drove his hips all the way up to his slobbering chin.

One down and two to go.

Mule was coming out of his chair. Slow, ponderous, he was raising like a cardiff giant. The other punk was closer and faster. He jumped at me. His mistake. He should have run. I shot the heel of my hand to his chin, cupped it there, stopping him in the middle of his rush until I got my fingers behind his lower lip. I hung onto that lower lip and drove my foot into his gut, hung onto it tore and split and slipped out of my bloody fingers as he jackknifed into the table, turned it over and fell on top of it.

Two down and one to go.

"Hi, Mule." Insane hate throbbing in my throat, the lust to rend and tear quivering every muscle in my body. "You're for dessert."

"I'm going to break you in two," he said flatly. He believed it. Apparently no man had ever stopped that ponderous strength of his.

"I'm going to let you try," I said softly, the madness jumping in me. "After you try, I'm going to break you up, piece by piece. Here's my hands, take them." I held them out to him, the cunning madness in me chuckling slyly.

He slapped his huge paws over them, his lips twisting in a murderous scowl. I didn't give him any time to close them. I turned my hands away from his palms, against his thumbs and fingers, threw my weight forward. My hands came free of his thick fingers, slid across the palms and fastened on his thick wrists.

"Your turn, Mule," I whispered, my eyes burning into his. "Get loose before I kick you in the belly."

He jerked against my hands, like a fish on the end of a line. I kicked, but his legs were too thick, too beefy. It didn't register. He grunted.

"My mistake, Mule," I said. "I thought there was something there. A man usually has something there."

He twisted at the hands, jerked, pulled me across the floor.

"What's the matter, Mule?" I asked in a throbbing whisper. "Getting old and weak? Here, I'll turn them loose."

I let go, flipped the fingers from my left hand into his right eye socket, gouged. He started cursing, kept cursing in a steady monotone. He let the eye water and bleed, opened both arms, lunged. I let him get those huge arms around me, but I lifted mine. Bent the right at the elbow, planted it in his throat. His tongue popped out. He floundered, fighting to suck air.

"Should I break your neck now, bastard? Like you broke Sheila's—and Kirk's? Or should I play with you a little?" He backed away, fighting for breath through his bruised windpipe.

"Let me see that finger, Mule." I grabbed the hand, ripped the bandage off. "Nice teeth marks. My teeth marks. You ditry murdering bastard!"

Control left me. I fought him like I fought the leather belts, the straitjackets, the six orderlies trying to hold me down. I let my rage and frustration pour out of me, with no straitjackets, no belts, no orderlies to stop me.

I slugged him until he slumped to his knees. Then I kicked him until he rolled over onto the floor ... In the face ... In the groin ... In his ears. He wouldn't knock out. He kept blubbering through the blood in his mouth. I stomped him in the kidneys, the shortribs. He kept groaning. I mashed his hands with my crushing heels.

"I'll break your neck now, Mule." I reached down and grabbed him by the hair, lifted his bloody head. "Wish you could tell me what it feels like when the bones break, when they start splintering and popping in your filthy skull."

I jerked him to a sitting position by his hair, stepped in back of him and rammed my knee between his shoulder blades, forcing his huge shoulders down on his knee caps. I held him there with my knee, placed my left hand on the back of his head, reached around his bloody cheek with my right hand and wrapped it around his shovel chin. I did it slow, careful, savoring each movement through the red, killing haze that gripped my gut. I twisted his big, blood-soppy head around until his pig eyes were popping, looking unseeingly into mine. Held the head at the spot where the spine was twisted as far as it would go, where another half-inch would pop it like a rotten limb.

CHAPTER FIFTEEN

A N UNEARTHLY WAILING BEAT FAINTLY AT MY EARS. It grew louder. And louder. I knelt there and held his head, not moving, listening intently to the strange sound. It beat at the red haze covering my senses, pierced the killing fog shrouding my brain. Reality came crashing back. The overturned table, the wrecked room, the two men lying in their blood, the popped eyes of Mule staring up into mine.

"Why should I wreck the rest of my life for this bastard?" I asked myself wonderingly. "Kirk's gone, Sheila's gone—if I kill him now, I'll go. Three for one. A sucker bet—with me being the sucker. Another time. With no witnesses. I can get him alone...." I let the unclean head slip from my fingers, stood up wearily, watching Mule fall over on his side.

"A sample, Mule," I said quietly. "Your friends the police are coming. But I'm coming for you, Mule. Maybe tomorrow, maybe tomorrow night, but I'm coming. You go hole up somewhere, some little room. Wait and sweat there until I find you. Here's one for the road, Mule, one for the road to hell." I stomped him squarely in the face.

I went out the door, over the fence, into the 'Bird, made a screeching U-turn in the street, gunned the 'Bird away from the loudly wailing siren, less than two blocks away. Burning rubber into the fast settling night, I cut the 'Bird into the slot, almost peeling paint from Mike's Cadillac, in back of my apartment. I went up the stairs two at a time.

From the front door I went into the bathroom. I had a bruise under my right eye, not too big and a thin cut in the middle of my forehead, half an inch below the hairline. My sportcoat fit loose. I pulled it off. It was torn at both armpits, split up the back. My shirt had blood spots scattered on it. I took it off, threw it and the coat in the wash hamper. I finished stripping, got under the shower then toweled down. Rapidly I slipped into an undershirt and shorts, then donned white shirt and string tie, dove-grey flannel suit, grey suede shoes with knitted socks.

The pounding on the front door started.

I checked the bathroom with a critical eye, kicked my tan shoes in back of the toilet bowl. Satisfied, I started for the front door.

The phone rang.

I paused. Decided to answer the phone first. I knew who was at the front door. Thought I knew who was on the phone, and I didn't want to talk in front of one to the other.

"Be there in a minute," I yelled at the front door.

"Open up!"

"Rest your flat feet, Hogarth," I yelled back. "I got a phone to answer."

I snatched the phone from the cradle.

"Call you back, Barb—" I started softly, then stopped.

"Roscoe Todd?" the metallic voice droned.

"Here," I half-snarled.

"The very last chance," the metallic blur said flatly.

"Not buying chances in your raffle. Go to hell."

"If you change your mind at any time, tell the lawyer you will have to hire," the metallic voice said.

"Lawyer?" I asked stupidly.

The empty hum of the phone wire began in my ear. I cradled the phone, half ran to the front door to save the hinges. Hogarth carried a lot of beef and it sounded like he was using all of it. I turned the key, twisted the knob. A uniformed policeman fell into the hall, fighting to catch his balance.

"Could have told us you were opening up," Hogarth snorted, walking in.

"Got a search warrant?" I put my hand on his chest, stopped him.

"Don't need one. In pursuit of a fugitive."

"I didn't see a fugitive run through here." I said coldly. "Stretching it kind of thin, aren't you?"

"May I come in?" he asked quietly.

"That's better," I said lightly. "Sure, come in and have a drink."

"Thanks," he said dryly, shutting the door. He walked down the short hall, looking into each room as he passed it. The cop watched me warily, a naked pistol in his hand.

"Better put it away." I motioned at the pistol, letting a smile come to my eyes. "Hogarth isn't playing cops and robbers any more. He's my guest, didn't you hear?"

"I seen those guys," the cop said flatly. "I'll keep it in my hand."

"Put it away," Hogarth said wearily from the living room entrance. "Come in here an sit down."

"Thanks," I said dryly. "You make a lovely hostess, Toots."

The cop holstered his pistol, stepped back to let me pass, followed me warily, his hand an inch from the gun butt.

"Hogarth," I said disgustedly, "tell this meathead to lay off before I bust his arm. He's still playing cops and robbers. If I do something that startles him and he makes a grab for that pistol, I'll have to bust his arm. Cop or no cop.

"Tough, ain'tcha?" Hogarth grunted. The three of us were standing in the living room.

"Just as tough as circumstances make me," I said flatly.

Hogarth waved his arm at the cop.

"Button it up," he said. "Wait in the hall. If this rough neck starts anything, you'll be safer. You'll have a chance to get your gun out and take one shot, anyway, before he gets his hands on you."

The cop sidled into the hall, not turning his back on me. He backed through the front door, closed it nervously.

"Okay," I said, sitting down on the sofa. "What brings you here?"

Hogarth spread his feet, put his hands on his hips.

"Explain that cut on your forehead," he growled.

"Let's see," I said. "Something's just a little wrong. I got it! You need a bowler hat and a cigar. And you should have tipped the bowler hat onto the back of your head before you put your hands on your hips. You've had bad instructions, Sergeant. The police school didn't quite give you the whole picture."

Hogarth scowled.

"That's better," I said happily. "Now you're working up to it. A few minutes more and we can start the cameras rolling."

"Let's start over," Hogarth said patiently, ignoring my remarks. "How did you get that cut on your forehead?"

"Shaving," I said.

"Yeah? With an electric razor?"

"Good eyes, Sergeant. You force me to raise your IQ."

"Let's start over again—"

"No, no, Sergeant," I said hastily. "We're wasting too much film. I was shaving when you started pounding on the door. I'm getting nervous lately, and what with that sudden pounding, my hand jumped. See? The razor hit here first. Made a bruise under my eye, then it glanced off and bit my forehead. Those things can get nasty sometimes. You scare them and they'll attack you something fierce."

"That's your story?" he asked quietly.

"Uh huh," I said. "As good a story as I can think of. You didn't give me much time."

"Keep telling them that then and you'll have plenty of time. Ten years of it." He eased his bulk onto the couch.

"You sure ruin a good picture," I said nastily.

"Huh?"

"Sitting on that couch," I snapped. "The other picture was much better. But you had to go and sit right on her belly?"

Hogarth cast a startled look at the couch, then his face flushed with anger.

"Cut the horseplay," he barked. "If you won't answer my questions here, I'll take you down and let you answer them with a light in your face."

"I answered your question, Sergeant. You got some more, maybe?"

"Yeah. Where were you in the last hour?"

"Want an itemized list? I was standing, walking, driving, washing, drinking, and—oh, yes—shaving."

"I asked you where?"

"Why, Sergeant, how silly of me. On mother earth, American continent, the part that is the United States, in the state of Kentucky. Pardon me, it's a Commonwealth. In Campbell County, City of Newport. That's where."

"Where in Newport?" he growled patiently.

"Why, in the Campbell County part of Newport. Is there any other?"

"Is that all I'm going to get?"

"From me," I answered shortly. "Get off your big ass and dig up your evidence. There is a law in this country that says a man does not have to bear witness against himself. Seems that all the lazy cops and lawmakers have never read it. Be different,

Sergeant. Go and find out what I've been doing, get some people to swear that it was me that did it. Go down and see the District Attorney and convince him that the people who swore to the warrant were twenty-one and in their right mind. After you get the warrant for my arrest, go get the sheriff or one of his deputies to serve me with the warrant. Until you do all that, get the hell out of my apartment and stay out."

"I can take you in right now," he said angrily.

"On what charge?"

"Suspicion of assault and mayhem," he snapped.

"Arrest me then. Right now. And hope to God that you can prove that suspicion, else I'll make it so hot for you you'll want to go back to walking a beat."

"You citizens!" he snorted. "All you self-righteous guys make the same threat. You really scare me, you do," he said sarcastically.

"So?" I said coldly. "Who in hell would try to scare a tub of lard like you? Ever hear of a suspension, Sergeant? For dereliction and improper use of authority? The minute your arrest on suspicion falls through—and you know damn well it will, or you would have come here with a warrant—I'll grab one of these shyster lawyers and charge you with every citizens outrage law that is written. I've got thirty thousand dollars that says I can make it stick."

Detective Sergeant Hogarth sat looking at me. His thin lips spread in a lopsided grin.

"I like you," he said, the lopsided grin spreading. "No, I respect you, you bullheaded Irisliman. You don't bluff worth a damn, you speak your piece. I know you're hell on wheels, but I can't prove it. In a way, I'm glad I can't. But I've got a job to do.

"Seems a man busted into a card game in a private house a little while ago," he continued. "He not only busted into the house—he busted up three men. One of them is in a pretty bad condition. Two mangled arms and a double rupture. Adam Costa—he's supposed to be a top muscle man in Newport—looks like he's been hit with a tank. Two hands chewed all to hell, features smeared all over his face, a couple of broken ribs and bleeding from the kidneys. Any other man take a beating like that and he'd be dead, but not this muscle punk. He didn't even want to go to the hospital. Also we found a drunken girl staggering around with no clothes on."

"Should I be interested?" I asked in a bored voice.

"Thought you might be," he said mildly. "I arrested them all. Got a pickup out on the man whose coat we found on the floor. Damn fool left his billfold in it. No one's talking yet. Don't think any of them will. That smart lawyer—Jerkins, you met him, he handles all these cases—will have them sprung from jail before morning, or outta custody. Hadda send all three to the hospital, if they wanted it or not. Took the drunken dame to the lockup."

"So?"

"So I'll be going now." He got up. "I know who did it, but like you say, it would be a lot of work to prove. Unless the man with the mangled arms dies, making it murder. Then I'll have to prove it. Hope he lives." He paused in the doorway. "Only one thing worries me. I wish that doc hadn't called me from the Naval hospital. Crazy people are hard to figure. If you're really nuts, I'm sticking my neck out."

"If I'm nuts, you'll owe that doc a few thank you's," I said shortly.

"For warning me to use a high powered rifle on you, I suppose?"

"Yeah," I said. "I'd hate like hell to wake up in a padded cell and have a headshrinker tell me that I'd torn you apart for the undertakers to piece together."

"I'd better leave before we start being palsy-walsy," he said dryly.

After he left, I lit a cigarette, went to the kitchen and opened a cold bottle of beer, went back to the living room and sprawled out on the sofa.

The boss had six men mangled—no, seven, counting the one from Chicago—and three of them run out of town. News of that sort travels fast in a set-up like the boss's. Also a write up in a local paper. Gambling empires break fast under that sort of pressure. So if I was the boss, what would I do? Why, I'd play my high card.

Sheila Thomson's murder.

There was a certain risk for the boss in that. Mule and the one they called Lefty would have to make a sworn statement. But after what happened to Big John, Tim, Jackson—and tonight Mule, Lefty—if the man was Lefty—and the knifer, they could make an airtight case.

They could say that they thought it was on business of theirs, that they didn't want to get mixed up with the police. But after what had happened, and after figuring me for a maniac, they had thought the police had better handle the matter.

If Hogarth got sold on the idea that all the beatings and riots were the result of my trying to shut up witnesses, he would come looking for me with that high-powered rifle. No jury would ever have a chance of weighing the evidence.

I still had no idea who the boss was. Setting me up like a clay pigeon, and I couldn't see the person behind the gun sights. There was still the possibility that the boss would try one last desperate chance to gang me. I didn't know how many men the boss commanded, or if a hired killer was on the plane for Newport at this moment—maybe already here and given his instructions.

So I didn't know from which direction the boss would strike but I knew the king rat would strike. From this moment I would have to live on my toes, keep moving, and watch. Watch for a mistake in the jungle attack. One mistake. If I ever got on the boss's trail, with a hot scent in my nostrils, it would take all his hired killers and the police to stop me—to stop me short of the boss's living body.

I put the cigarette out, got up from the sofa, went into the bedroom and took five hundred dollars out of the dresser drawer. If I needed it, I didn't want to be caught without money for cab, plane, or train fare. I went down to the 'Bird, backed it from the slot and headed for the Barby. I wanted to see if Big John and his sidekicks had cleared. If they hadn't, I was going to clear them, even if I had to load them in the 'Bird like wet sacks and dump them in a loose boat on the Ohio River.

CHAPTER SIXTEEN

T he Barby was quiet. The barkeep poured me a shot of White Horse impersonally.

"How's the games going?" I asked.

"No games tonight," he said shortly.

"What, no suckers to dump their money?" He was the same barkeep that had put the card in front of me earlier.

"No one to take the suckers' money," he said sourly, looking at me hard. "You wouldn't know about that, huh?"

"About what?"

"About them checking out of their apartment." He grinned suddenly. "Seems they got busted up some. The landlady told the guy I sent up there after they didn't answer their phone that they were in an awful shape when they left. What've you got against them guys, anyway?"

"Nothing. Not any more. But if you happen to see them around, tell them they goofed their last chance. Tell them the guy with the doll face said it." I downed my scotch.

As I set the glass down, my nerves tingled. My back was to the door, but the smell carried to me, waves of soft, pleasing stink. I knew before I turned slowly around that I would see her. I wanted to see her while she was standing, before she lowered that lovely body of hers into a chair.

As I turned, she was standing just in the doorway. Her lovely dark eyes were watching me. Her sooty black hair lay in soft curls, with a diamond tiara, a different diamond tiara. This one was a gold snake, with emerald eyes. She wore no earrings on her shell pink ears, no necklace on her soft white throat, no pendant between the soft white mounds of flesh. The sheer black dress she wore revealed every curve, every dimple. Even the dimple at the navel. She walked towards me, her eyes on mine. She leaned lightly against the bar.

"Whiskey straight," she said to the barkeep. She waited, leaning on the bar and looking up into my face. The barkeep set the glass down, poured the drink. She picked it up, her eyes still locked on mine, downed the drink, set the glass down.

"I'm not that good-looking," she said softly. "You look like you want to eat me."

"If I started eating you, I'd get arrested."

"Arrested? What if I didn't complain?" She smiled slightly.

"Wouldn't have to," I said promptly. "The boys from the Pure Food Administration would get me for spoiling good meat."

She laughed. It floated all through her, causing her breasts to swell, the pulse in her throat to beat, dimples to show in the smooth cheeks.

"The way you are now, all I want to do is look at you, all night then see what the early light from the morning sun would turn you into," I said, wanting to lay a hand on her creamy shoulder.

"Probably turn me into a hag," she said lightly.

"Never," I said gravely.

"If you keep talking that nice, I'll let you sit with me."

"My honor," I said, bowing slightly from the waist. "Yours to command."

She grinned a gamin grin and walked over to a table by the wall, waited by the chair for me to seat her. I brushed the back of her neck with my lips as she sat down.

"Ah-ah!" she laughed. "Remember the Pure Food laws!"

"You owe me an apology," I said sternly, sitting down and leaning my elbows on the table.

"You? Why?" She made those brown eyes big.

"For bumping your neck into my lips when you sat down. They're bruised. I'm sure that if my mother were here, she would kiss them to take the hurt away."

"Your mother wouldn't even kiss you with that mustache!" she teased.

"She would—if she was as young as you are."

"And you wouldn't mind—if she was as pretty as I am?"

"Pretty? You? What makes you think you're pretty?"

"Why I—you're impossible," she said with a frown. "I said that you could sit with me only if you talked nice."

"Then don't call yourself pretty. It's a disgrace." I grinned with my eyes. "You're beautiful, lovely, wonderful. Pretty doesn't do you justice."

"I do declare!" she mocked. "I bet you know poetry!"

"The poetry of beauty I know," I said softly, letting my eyes get hot. "I love to look at it, feel it—possess it."

"You'd better be a looking poet right now," she warned. "I'm thirsty."

"Water or lemonade?" I asked innocently.

"Either one. As long as it has a good whiskey chaser."

"Water!" I called to the barkeep. "With one whiskey and one scotch chaser. Just a little water with a big chaser," I added.

"I'm afraid I got a big chaser at the table already," she said with a smile.

"Don't let it bother you now," I said. "Just which chaser finally puts you to sleep."

"You'd better watch that none of these men around here doesn't put you to sleep," she warned meaningfully.

"They're welcome to try any time," I said dryly, watching her closely. Her tie-in with the gang could be very possible. I wouldn't mind. I was trying all the angles, even if they were curves. "What do you mean by that crack? Got a husband or somebody around to get you out of trouble?"

"I'm sorry," she said, twisting her fingers. The barkeep put the order on the table. She downed hers quickly. I sipped at mine.

"Sorry about what?" I asked, curious.

"I'd better warn you," she said, pulling a cigarette from her case. I lit it. "Everytime I get too friendly with a man, somebody beats him up."

"Why?"

"I don't know," she said miserably. "All of them have made passes at me some time or the other. I think they get jealous if I favor someone else."

"Nuts," I said, but didn't mean it. More likely she belonged to some member of the gang and didn't know it. And if she did know it, enjoyed the fighting over her.

"Hey!" I said, suddenly remembering. "In case you're interested, I'm Roscoe Todd. You can call me Toddy, among other things."

"Among what other things?" she asked scornfully.

"Like darling, lover, honey, sweetheart," I said airily.

"Not bastard, masher, sonofabitch or ———?" The last word jarred me. She grinned a gamin grin as she noticed it.

"Poison dripping from a petal of a rose," I said harshly.

"What did you expect?" She rested her chin in her cupped hand, elbow on table. "I'm a girl and I get around. So relax, Loverboy, and tell me what you want. You can call me Stella, among other things. But the name is Mrs. Stella Spigota. Don't blame the Spigota on me. That happens to be the name of the jerk I married.

For your information, I'm still married, but not very much." She signaled the barkeep for another round.

"Married—but not very much? My luck, picking the married ones." I looked at her blandly, turning the scotch slowly in my fingers.

"Not very much is your good luck, maybe," she said. "It's all in the way you ask." The barkeep set our drinks down, left. "Not drinking, Lover-boy? I'm a heavy one up." She raised the glass in a half salute, downed the double shot neatly.

"All in the way I ask what?" I downed my scotch, shoved the empty to the side, curled my fingers around the replacement. If she kept the pace, neither one of us would be in a condition to ask anything.

Stella was feeling the three fast ones. Her eyes were hazy, softer, her motions more languid. She leaned over the small table, her low-cut black dress framing the soft mounds teasingly. She tapped me lightly on the knuckles with her fingertips. She noticed the bruised and tender skin, the result of various contacts with Mule.

"What does a man usually ask a girl he picks up in a bar?" she asked cryptically.

"You asked me, so I'll answer," I said flatly. "You like to sleep single or double?"

"I like to sleep single—but play double," she answered tartly, and in the same breath. "From the looks of those knuckles, you like to brawl, Mister."

"More interested in sleeping double—or, as you put it—playing double." If she was on the make, I was interested in getting made.

"Oh, go to hell," she said crossly. "You damn men always have your mind in your pants."

"Yeah," I said slowly, anger at her kind starting to burn and mix with disgust. "But all I've been doing is trying to show you a good time. You're the one that's been leading with the dirt."

To hell with her, I thought; the Boat Club is doing business by now. I wanted to see what kind and how I could interrupt it, not sit bantering meaningless smut with a lovely but drunk dame.

"Thanks, Baby, for an uninteresting ten minutes," I said quietly, shoving my chair back.

"I'm not very interesting, am I?" she said dejectedly. "I'm sorry. I never was very good at playing the gay girl. That's why I sit around all night and drink." She wasn't putting on an act. Deep loneliness was in the brown eyes, with a touch of bitterness and self-pity. "Go away, fella. You're the same as the rest. The girl doesn't talk smutty and toss her behind around, make out like she wants to crawl in bed with you, you got no use for her. If she does talk and throw her behind around like she wants it good and you're not in the mood, you still got no use for her." Her eyes lit with scorn. "I don't need to cadge your drinks. Take this five-dollar bill and pay the barkeep." She dug into her tiny purse, ripped out the bill. "You can keep the change for your trouble."

I pulled the chair back to the table, took her hand with the five-dollar bill in it in both my hands.

"So I'm wrong about you, Stella," I said. Maybe the kid was all mixed up about men. I knew I was all mixed up about girls. Why did I have to jump to conclusions about her—about Barby? A girl acts friendly and I start thinking that she's a member of the gang, that she's a no good bitch. The low opinion I had of myself was caused by looking too much in a mirror, back at the Naval Hospital. How do I know where a girl gets an opinion about herself? Maybe by watching the lewd light in a man's eyes.

"I'm sorry," I continued. "Let's start over again. I don't need a girl for my bed. I could get one in five minutes in this joint." I waved my hand at four of the blue jean set, elbows hooked over the bar, hips bent out like lazy mares at the hitching post.

"You mean you don't want to go to bed with me?" she snapped angrily, jerking her hand from mine. "Look, fella, that's the only thing I got that I was sure someone would want. If you don't want that, what in hell do you want?"

"Maybe I just want to sit and talk. Listen to you and look at you. Can you tell me one good reason for *that* being the only thing that boy meets girl for?"

"That's the only thing I can think of right now," she said sullenly. "And mister, if you don't think that's the only reason why boy meets girl in this dump, you've been drinking too much or have just escaped from a prayer meeting."

"Maybe we had better change to some other place," I said, letting my eyes smile. "But not to a prayer meeting. That'd be carrying it too far."

She grinned at me.

"Maybe you're all right, Doll. Maybe I never met a guy like you before. I got nothing to lose," she said candidly. "Not even my husband. I can't lose him, no matter how hard I try." She tilted back her head and laughed.

"Something funny?"

She stopped laughing, but continued to smile, a taunting shadow in her eyes. "Would you care to buy a fifth and take me home? My husband won't get home until two or three o'clock. He works nights."

"What's so funny about that? My taking you home—your husband working nights?"

"I was thinking of the look on that smooth face of yours when I introduce you to him." She had the gamin grin again.

"You're either nuts or drunk," I said flatly, getting up from the table.

"Afraid?" she laughed.

"Hell no," I snapped. "But damned if I take you home and wait for your husband to catch me there. Of all the crazy ideas, that's the most."

"What's so wrong with it?" she asked, standing up. "We aren't going to do anything but talk and drink a few highballs. You said a minute ago that all you wanted to do is listen to me and look at me. You said that you wanted to go some place else. Can you think of a better place?"

"There is such a thing as convention," I said weakly.

"My husband is from France. He doesn't think anything has to be wrong because somebody thinks it's wrong. Conventions are for the spineless jerks anyway." She stood close, looking up into my face, the soft white body in the black sheer dress inviting and pulsing tantalizingly. "Will you get the fifth?"

"Why not? I can walk out anytime I want to," I said quietly. "Scotch or whiskey?"

"Get both," she said pertly, tossing her head. "When I finish the whiskey I can help you on the scotch."

"You drink that much and you won't be able to introduce me to your husband," I warned, paying fifteen dollars for eight bucks worth of bottles.

"You mean that I'll pass out?" She grinned her gamin grin. "Or are you just hoping?"

"Nope," I said, taking her by the arm and heading for the 'Bird. "I get no kicks from a drunken dame."

"I've been told that I'm very beautiful—and very desirable when I'm passed out," she said mockingly as I seated her in the car.

Our talk consisted of her telling me how to get to her house. Through Newport to Licking Pike, out the Licking Pike to Wilder, then some twists and turns in a subdivision. She finally told me to stop in front of a new ranch house, half hidden by trees and evergreen bushes. I had to stop anyway, because we were at the end of the pavement.

"Nice isolated place you have," I commented.

"Ummm," she said. "No prying neighbors."

She jumped out of the car and went up the walk with the two bottles in her hands. I followed, waited while she fumbled for her key, finally took the bottles before she dropped them.

"Sure we got the right house?" I whispered hoarsely. I didn't know how drunk this dame could be. She had three before we left. How many she had before she came in was anybody's guess. Light clouds were racing across the moon and the night was still and quiet, with insects and frogs cheeping and croaking in subdued chants. A drunken dame and an unreal night. What in hell was I doing here, waiting for a strange girl to open a strange door, holding two bottles of hard stuff in my hands? With those thin broken clouds racing across the moon when no wind could be felt. Taking every path, I answered myself, hoping that one of them would lead me to the boss—but I had a feeling that this path was going to lead me to a bed.

"Of course this is the right house," Stella whispered to answer my question. "Silly. There, see? I finally found the right key. Come on in," she whispered anxiously.

"Sure, it's all right?" I whispered back.

"Of course," she whispered impatiently. "Oh, damn, you've even got me doing it!" she said suddenly in a loud voice. She flipped on a wall switch, pulled me by an arm through the door. "What do you want to do, stand out there all night? It's much nicer in here." She laughed and kicked off her shoes. "Kick yours off, too, if your feet don't stink."

"I've heard it said that when a girl takes off her shoes, she's ready to take off other things, too," I said lightly.

"You heard right," she said promptly. "Go in the kitchen and find some glasses and ice. Take your coat and tie off, make yourself comfortable. That's what I'm going to do." She disappeared through an archway.

I set the bottles down on a coffee table, looking the large room over. It had a big stone fireplace, paneled walls, those screwy paintings, all colors, circles and squares. There was a picture window with draw drapes, assortment of end tables, big comfortable chairs, little uncomfortable chairs, sofa, couch, potted imitation flowers, wall to wall carpet. The room was done in tan and gold and rose. Interior decorator's job ... Professional.

I sat on one of the little hard chairs and took off my shoes, coat and tie. Right in the middle of the big, coldly professional room, feeling like I was undressing in the lobby of the Waldorf. I got up and chose the door on my left, hoping to find the kitchen, but found myself in a shadowy dining room, also with a thick rug. Probably the kitchen had a thick rug, too. It didn't. The tile was cold on my feet. I found the light switch, flipped it on.

Modern kitchen ... All cabinets ... Couldn't tell the stove from the sinktop ... Everything covered up ... Porcelain and nickelplate. I opened what I thought was the refrigerator and discovered it was the washing machine. Trying again I got the garbage disposal. A man could starve to death before he found the food.

"Got the glasses and ice yet?" Stella called from somewhere in the other end of the house.

"Can't find the damn refrigerator."

"It's the big door to your right where the row of windows end." I heard her distant laugh of amusement.

Built in, so I pulled at the sunken handle, then decided I had to push it. The door popped open. Never saw such an assortment of cooked food stuffed in one place in my life. And I mean stuffed. Some of it spilled out on the floor and I had to jam it back in.

I kept opening doors until I found some glasses and a big bowl. I dumped the bowl full of ice cubes, jammed some more cooked food back into the refrigerator, picked up the bowl of ice and the glasses and went back into the living room. After packing ice cubes in two glasses, I poured one full whiskey and one full of scotch. I sat down in one of the large comfortable chairs, put my feet on a footstool, and took a good pull at the scotch.

Stella came into the room. I almost spilled what was left of the scotch. She had made herself comfortable, but the black lacy negligee made me uncomfortable. One of those kind where you can see more when it's on than when it's off. She also had the diamond tiara out of her hair. It took me a minute to notice that.

She picked her glass up and I watched as the liquid went down her throat, into her chest all silky smooth flowing movements. She set the glass down, lifted my feet over the footstool and sat down facing me.

"Now let's talk," she said brightly, lacing her fingers around one bare knee.

"Huh?" I said stupidly.

"Talk. You know, be different. You said you just wanted to sit, talk and look at me." She smiled sweetly, stretched her arms wide, twisted back and forth from the hips. What that did to the negligee was out of this world. I was, too.

CHAPTER SEVENTEEN

"How do i look?" she asked teasingly.

So help me, I wanted to answer that, but my heart was knocking around too much. It felt like it was my throat, in my stomach, jumping from one side to the other. The way my head was throbbing, it felt like it had even got up there.

"Maybe you don't care so much about talking? Want to relax a little bit?" she asked softly, leaning forward and placing her hands on my knees, arms supporting her shoulders.

I leaned forward and set the scotch glass gently on the rug. That brought her face within inches of mine. She didn't pull back. I looked deep into those soft brown, suddenly still eyes. I took her arms at the wrists, felt the hot white flesh quiver as my hands moved up, up over the white dimpled elbows, onto the soft shoulders. The heat from my eyes set hers to burning. Slowly, her tongue, pink and pointed, came out and moistened her suddenly quivering lips. Her eyes turned into two glowing, smoldering embers.

My hands wandered gently over her hot flesh, tearing absently at the negligee, moving it aside to get at the yielding flesh. Her arms lifted, her hands slipped eagerly up the back of my neck.

Then I was looking down, her head framed by the pillow, and the world could wait. She tilted her head back on the pillow, pulled my lips down to hers again. Her mouth was open, seeking. A wildness ran through her, grabbed me in its frenzy. She tugged hungrily at my shoulders, pulled me over.

"It's been a long time," she said, much later, tracing circles on my chest with one tiny finger.

"How long?" I had a notion what she was talking about.

"Over three months." She nuzzled my neck with her lips.

"You mean since a man?"

"Uh huh. Every man I get always gets beat up. He does everything but run the next time he sees me." She pushed me away. "I think the damn Frenchman has it done. Oh, he never says anything to me. He's a sneaky bastard."

"Tell him to call out the army at Ft. Knox," I said dryly. "If he's going to chase me, he'll need it."

"I know all about you and those tough guys at the Barby. The whole town knows about it. Why do you think I made a play for you?" She laughed. "I said to myself: if you can get that hunk of man, the damn Frenchman won't have a chance to scare him off. So—," she ran her fingers over my chest muscles, "—now I got you, lover."

"Sure, there wouldn't be a little gambling mixed up in it somewhere, Beautiful?" I asked sharply.

"Gambling?" She appeared startled. "What do you mean by that? You mean cards and dice, stuff like that? I don't know a damn thing about that sort of thing. Just what do you mean?" Her brown eyes had definite storm signals showing.

"Whoa now, Honey. Whoa." I grabbed her in my arms and rolled her over, held her tight, rubbed her nose with mine. "Can't a guy ask a question without you getting all riled up?"

"Not about gambling," she said, squirming under my weight. "The Frenchman is always making sly remarks about gambling. I know damn well he doesn't make the kind of money he has by waiting table."

"What kind of remarks he make?"

"He's always talking about guys that'd like to meet me," she said spitefully. "I think the guys he always talks about would like to 'meat' me, but not the way he thinks. But then I don't think he'd give a damn, so long as he could make some money."

"You ever find out how he makes his money?" I asked, biting her ear. She tried to get the ear away, finally held still.

"He's always hinting about gambling," she said, her mind no longer on what she was saying. "But when I come out and ask him, he grins real silly. One time he took me to the Terrace Plaza and a wealthy looking man came over to the table. He made some remark about my being more than welcome at any game. The Frenchman got nervous and started talking about something else. Stop it!" She wriggled her whole body.

"Stop what?" I asked, my voice muffled.

"You can't do both at the same time," she gasped. "Either stop talking or—or stop that!" She bit me on the ear.

"Why were you at the Barby tonight?" I raised myself on my elbows, looked down into her flushed face.

"To meet you," she said candidly. "I saw you the other night, just before you went into the back rooms and the riot started. After it was all over and I saw those two beat up men—they had them out on the sidewalk, the cops, that is—and the men wouldn't say anything, but the waitress started to say something and some punk told her to shut her trap. But she said enough so that I knew that it was you that did it. I decided that you were the man for me. Glad I did?" she asked, moving suggestively.

"Uh huh. By the way, where is the bathroom? I don't want to wander around all night in this ranch looking for it."

"Out the door. In the hall, silly."

"Thought it might be built in, like your kitchen. Pull a handle and have it slide out, maybe."

"What time did you say your Frenchman comes home?" I asked as I walked back into the bedroom.

"Around two o'clock. Why?"

I grabbed my clothes. "It's one thirty now, Darling. I wouldn't want him to catch me with my pants down," I said, dressing fast.

"Oh, damn," Stella said. "How the time flies when you're enjoying yourself." She got up, rummaged in a closet, came out with a slightly less transparent negligee, put it on.

"Let's go out to the living room and have a drink. I need it," she said, going out the door with the negligee trailing back from those trim white legs.

"To us," she said, raising the glass, the ice cubes we had rescued from the water in the bowl glinting in the light. "And many more nights together."

"Also," I said and downed my drink.

She set her empty glass down, came over and shoved me into the comfortable chair, piled onto my lap.

"Tomorrow night, Darling, I want to hear all about you. Your first girl, why you aren't married—" she stopped. "You aren't married, are you?" she asked.

"Huh uh. Not me. But right now I'm worrying about your husband walking in that door with you sitting like this." I patted her bare leg where the negligee had fallen away.

For an answer she put her arms around my neck, pulled herself high on my chest, tilted my head back and kissed me, a long, open-mouthed kiss.

"Do that again—," I said hoarsely, "—and your husband will catch us in the bedroom."

"Think I'd care?" she said, smiling, but got up from my lap. "Better go in the bathroom and get rid of my lipstick. You look like an Indian painted up for a war dance."

As I finished washing, I heard a car pull up outside, the car door slam, and the car pull away. I walked out into the living room. Someone was unlocking the front door. Stella was draped over the armchair, her bare legs dangling, a look of scorn forming on her beautiful face as she watched the door. It opened.

"Hello," the man said, pushing his way in, a bundle under his arm. "Warm out tonight." He dumped the bundle in a chair, looked at me.

I knew it was the Frenchman. More, he was the same Frenchman that had waited on Barby and me out at Beverly Hills. He didn't act like he recognized me. Stella was looking at the bundle in the chair.

"More garbage from the tables?" she asked sullenly.

"It's good food, Stella. Why should I throw it away? Who is your friend, Stella?" He pronounced Stella as Stel-law.

"Mr. Todd to you, Frenchman."

"Glad to know you, Mr. Todd," he said, sticking out a pudgy hand. "Me, I'm Adrian Spigota. Everybody calls me Frenchy." He talked in a wheezy, apologetic voice.

"Glad to know you," I said, taking the pudgy hand. It felt like a ball of wet plaster. I dropped it.

"Let's all have a drink," he said anxiously, sitting down and pulling off his shoes. He wriggled his toes. "Feels good after standing all night."

"Go to bed," Stella said crossly. "We can have a drink without you and your stinking feet lousing it up."

"Aw, Stellaw," he said, looking at her with those soft calf eyes. "Didn't you have a good time tonight?"

"Wouldn't you like to know!" she said spitefully, kicking her feet high, showing much too much of her white body. "Why didn't you let some whiskey out, Fatty? Mr. Todd had to buy it for us."

"I didn't know Mr. Todd was coming," he said plaintively. "Next time I let some out, Mr. Todd. Stellaw drinks too much when she's alone," he offered in apology.

"It's all right, Mr. Spigota," I said lamely, wishing I was out of the house.

He got up from the chair, let his breath out with a whoosh. I smelled garlic.

"I'm tired," he said in a wheedling voice. "I think I go to bed. You don't mind, Mr. Todd?"

"Not at all. I must be going, anyway."

"That's all right," he said, picking up his bundle and padding towards the kitchen. "You stay as long as you want. I sleep tight. Your talking won't bother me."

I heard him opening the refrigerator, stuffing the food in. The door closed with a snap. I heard him shuffling into the bedroom. Stella made an obscene motion with her hand and patted her belly.

"You poor bastard," she said in his direction.

"I'd better be going," I said again and headed for the door. Stella scrambled off the chair, threw her arms around my neck.

"Wait a few minutes," she said, not bothering to whisper. "He'll be asleep then. I'd like to use the sofa while he's snoring. Don't you think it would be fun?"

"With the noise you make?" I asked, genuinely startled. "He'd wake up even if I hit him in the head with a bottle. No thanks."

"I'll go out to the car with you," she offered.

"You'll stay right here," I said sternly, taking her arms from around my neck. "There's other times and other nights, Darling. Let's not ruin them."

"Is that a promise?" she asked softly. "You'd change any of your plans—or your work—for more nights with me?"

"It's a promise," I said, not daring to think what that question might mean. Time for that later.

"I think I'll sleep out here on the sofa," she said unhappily. "I don't want to get in bed with that tub of lard. Don't you think he's a queer or something? Not even raising his voice when he found me here with you—like this?" She undid the belt on the negligee, flapped it wide. "He's certainly not a man," she said scornfully.

"He's a queer one at that," I said uneasily. Stella was Stella and the Frenchman was the Frenchman, but that didn't help the bad taste in my mouth. But the taste in my mouth wasn't strong enough to stop the white rip of desire that went through me at the sight of her white, dimpled body. She pulled the negligee together again, tied the ribbon that passed for a belt.

"Just testing," she said, that gamin grin on her lips again. "He's snoring already. Listen!"

His breath was ripping in and out, tearing at his tonsils and adenoids.

"The sofa is real comfortable," she said, running her tongue over dry lips. "I'm going to sleep there anyway."

She undid the ribbon, slipped out of the negligee, let it fall. She took my two nerveless hands and placed them on her soft body, pressed herself against me. They say hell has no fury like a woman scorned. I decided on rubbery legs that this wasn't the time to find out.

Rotten, rotten to the core. I put the key into the switch, twisted the 'Bird into life, backed around, let the 'Bird idle along the street. Rotten, I said to myself again, thinking of Stella as I had left her, sleeping peacefully on the sofa. No doubt about it, the boss was throwing flesh in my way, gobs of it. All of it beautiful. I hated to think of Barby being part of it. Stella's kind I could see, but Barby—To hell with it, I wanted a good hot shower, a tumble in the hay, alone this time. But the facts kept coming back; Barby button-holes me on the Boat Club, makes a point of going to Beverly Hills, where she must be seated at a certain table, where this Frenchman waits on us, trying to fill a ridiculous order. Then I got to sample the fleshpot, with all I wanted in the future.

Stella snares me in the Barby, smears the fleshpot all over me, with a promise for the future, but with almost a direct question. The same Frenchman comes home as her husband, doesn't mind me a bit.

Only one thing good about it; it was much better wrestling the girls than it was the men—I gunned the 'Bird viciously, burned rubber for my apartment.

The snares were all around me. When they had been set and if they would be changed only time could tell. A very short time, after what had happened to some of the gang tonight. No gang boss would go on amusing me while I tore his—or her—empire to shreds, made cripples of his best men.

But the boss had offered me a job—offered it to me twice, hinted that it would be open indefinitely. Was the boss trying to make it so inviting that I couldn't refuse? Look at the boss's side of it: would a man like me on the team be worth six—or even sixteen—of his best men? Judging by the monkeys I'd made of his men, I had to admit that he would be making a good trade.

Barby, Stella—how many more wonderful fleshpots could the boss toss in my way? What a life to lead. That Barby or Stella amounted to anything more than come-ons was doubtful. The boss wouldn't let anyone in the know get too close to me. Or would he? Something kept nudging the back of my tired brain.... I decided to hell with it, tomorrow was another day. If I could stay awake until I got into the shower, that would be enough. Didn't want the 'Bird twisted around my neck.

CHAPTER EIGHTEEN

I STRIPPED IN THE BEDROOM, went into the bathroom, turned both shower faucets all the way, plunged under the hissing, wild water.

Me, I thought idly, feeling the jetted water sting and bite, I'm the same as this water: driving, stinging, restless, turned loose and running wild, out of control. I hoped, toweling myself down ruthlessly, I'd do the same as the water: cleanse before I found the final drain and slipped down into the oblivion of nature's processes.

I applied the nutrient oil generously, ran a comb through my tightly curled hair, trimmed the hairline above my lip. Brushed my teeth, straightened the bathroom, dried the floor with the damp towel, tossed it into the clothes hamper. The shower had driven the relaxed drowsy numbness from my body, left it pleasantly tired. I walked into the bedroom and admired the downy softness of the fourposter.

The telephone rang. Insistent.

I went into the living room, jerked the receiver from the cradle.

"Who in the hell—," I snarled into the mouthpiece, "—has the gall to call this time in the morning? Go to hell until after breakfast!"

"Toddy!" The voice was sharp. I halted the phone on the way to the cradle.

"Barby?"

"Yes, Darling, your Barby." I heard her sigh of relief. "You sounded like you thought it was the devil himself."

"I'm sorry, but I'm tired. A bed is one of the most beautiful things I can think of at this moment."

"I've been calling you since ten o'clock," she said impatiently. "You must have just got home. I've got to see you right away."

"Now, Honey, it's only been a matter of twenty-four hours since I last saw you," I said with a laugh in my throat. "Surely you can't be hurting again?"

The rippling laugh that came over the wire carried a pretty picture with it.

"Silly, that isn't what I want to see you about. Of course, after you get here and see this shorty nightgown I'm wearing, you might get interested. But I'm serious, Darling. I heard something tonight when I was in the Frontier Bar. You know how those booths are arranged? I'm sitting in one of them and some characters are sitting in the next.

"They were talking about you, and what they said scared me. If I hadn't read this evening's paper, I wouldn't have thought so much about it. Please, Darling, please come right over."

"Can't it keep until morning? I'm dog-tired."

"I have a bed," she said softly. "The way I feel right now, I'd like for you to use it. I mean the bed, Darling, not necessarily me. I've been sitting here all night, watching that crazy moon with the clouds shooting across it, with the night so still and muted, with what those men said running through my mind. I guess I'm scared, Darling. Scared because of you. Please don't say I'm silly. I want you near me for awhile. Maybe those crazy clouds racing across the moon would be romantic, instead of—of eerie, if you were here."

"You have a real case of jitters," I said with a laugh. "Those clouds racing across the moon are caused by a sky wind. But it is spooky—it made me feel spooky for awhile tonight, even if I had seen it a hundred times in the Pacific."

"Please come over. It's not far. You don't know it, but I live only five blocks from you. Go down to fourth, turn left and three blocks on the left is one of those big fancy brick houses. I'm sitting all alone in it on the second floor. Please?"

"Five blocks? Sounds more like ten to me, but what is the number?"

"It's 364—but don't bother to ring the front bell. Turn the knob as far as it will go to the left and the door will open. I hate carrying keys around with me, so I had a locksmith fix the door that way."

"Okay," I said. "But it'll be a few minutes. I'll have to put some clothes on."

"Don't bother on account of me," she said with an intimate giggle. "I'm not going to dress for you."

"I think maybe I'd better," I said dryly. "I might run into some other girl on the way, then I'd never get to see you tonight."

"Don't undersell, Darling." Barby laughed softly. "I'll go any girl's fee one better."

"You're a mink," I said flatly. "But right now I love minks. I'm coming over to have a serious talk with you, Mink. I wonder if it's a waste of time to talk seriously with a mink?"

"Not with this mink," Barby said, suddenly serious. "Please hurry."

Minks—I thought, dressing—at the rate I was going, I would have a mink ranch in another week, or my hide would be nailed to the mink fence to dry. Sobering thought.

Barbara Medina's house was easy to find. It sat back from the street, surrounded by tall shrubs and big elm trees. A massive, quiet building, with turreted roofs over twin towers reaching up to tickle the windswept stars, the heavy oaken shutters anchored tight against the solid brick walls, the windows massive, heavy and high. As I walked wearily up the steps to the big double doors, I half-expected to see a knight in chain mail lower his lance to block my way.

I took one of the big brass doorknobs and twisted it. Nothing happened. Barby said keep twisting, so I did. Two full turns later I heard the latch click. Neat. Like a combination on a banker's safe. The door opened noiselessly and I walked into a reception hall as big as my living room, with a wide, dark and shiny stairway sweeping in a half-circle up into the dim light before losing itself in the darkness above. A grandfather clock thwacked and thwocked monotonously against one wall. I shut the heavy door, waited, but couldn't hear a sound except the clock.

"Barby?" I said aloud, stifling an impulse to shout. Lucky I had. The 'Barby' continued to hang in the reception hall, then gloated graciously off and traveled around the house, repeating at each door its quiet summons.

If I was a jumping man, I would have jumped ten feet into the air and come down running. The lights came on that sudden. A chandelier, made of cut crystals anchored high in the ceiling, blazed into a million shimmering shards of white light.

"Hello, Darling."

I looked to the first landing on the wide stairway. Two small bare feet, toenails painted red, trim slender ankles, tapering into smooth rounded knees, swelling out into softly rounded white thighs, blended into a shimmering pale, gossamer thin garment that was clinging hesitantly to the softly rounded body until it had to cling desperately to the pointed, high breasts. Cling desperately because it ended just above the pointed, high breasts. Cling desperately because it ended just above the pointed mounds, with not enough pressure holding it there to dent the swelled flesh.

"You going to stare all night?" Barby laughed almost soundlessly. "Come up and inspect at closer range, but don't sneeze."

"I won't sneeze," I promised as I took the steps two at a time. "Whatever that is that you're wearing would look better cuddled up around your neck than laying on the floor."

Barby turned and skipped down a carpeted hall, entered a lighted doorway, paused to let me see the effect of the light through the garment, then jumped hastily into the room as I made a grab and missed. She draped herself into an armchair, legs dangling over one arm, back against the other, her bottom resting on the cushion, her right arm hooked over the back. She blew me a kiss with her left hand.

"Sit down, Darling," she said. I looked at her closely. The green eyes were serious. I sat down, using the side of her soft pink and satin bed.

"I didn't call you over here to—that is ..." She stopped abruptly, shook her long coppery hair defiantly. "Oh, damn, I mean I didn't call you over here just to go to bed with you. There, now does that clear the air a little?"

"If you don't want to go to bed with me, you'd better wrap a blanket around that part of you below your neck—fast," I warned.

"I didn't say that I didn't want to," she said demurely. "I said that it wasn't the only reason I called you. There is a difference, isn't there?"

"There must be, but right now I can't think of what it could be. I can't think, period." Thanks to Stella, she wasn't registering that bad, not quite.

She laughed softly, the laugh turning into a troubled frown.

"I'm worried about you, Toddy," she said earnestly. "I read that article in the paper yesterday. I tried to get you on the phone and when I couldn't, I started to look for you. I went to the Boat Club, stayed about an hour. Then I took a chance you might be at the Frontier Bar. I went into a booth and ordered a gin straight. While I was waiting to be served, I overheard some men talking in the next booth. I didn't really listen, not until I heard your name mentioned."

"What were they saying? Threatening to tie me in knots and ship me C.O.D. to the morgue?" I asked.

Her green eyes were fixed on me. Her face was still, troubled. Absently she hitched the filmy garment higher on one breast.

"Are you the Maniac? The one from Tacoma Beach?"

A pulse in her throat was jumping, otherwise she was immobile, one hand still, suspended in the act of hitching the garment higher, The thocking of the clock in the reception hall became loud. Easy, I told myself, easy does it. You have been expecting this, but not from her, not from Barby. Treat it lightly …

"Sure," I said easily, letting my eyes smile. "I'm just waiting for you to say no."

"I'm serious, Toddy. I heard one of those men say that the police would never doubt their statement that they saw you murder that girl at Tacoma. It—it scared me silly." She shivered.

"No," I said, getting up and walking over to the window. I stood watching the crazy moon, fighting to escape the sky driven winds, hurrying to nestle in the horizon before the sun came up and gobbled it. "No, I didn't kill that girl at Tacoma Beach. But I would like to know what those men looked like. Did you recognize any of them?"

"One of them—that is—I think I know one of them." She frowned. "He was beat up pretty bad and one eye was swelled closed, but I'm fairly sure he was that big guy that runs the gambling at the Boat Club. The one you asked about when I first met you."

"Mule?" I prompted.

"Yes, Mule," she said slowly. "But I couldn't swear it was him. The Frontier Bar is not too well lighted, and they were in a big hurry when they left."

"What did the others look like?"

"One was small and thin. He had on a dark suit. One of them was short, husky. He had his chin taped up."

"That's Mule, Lefty, and the lawyer," I mused aloud. "What about the fourth one?"

"He was short and sloppy fat. I only saw his back because he must have gone to the men's room or out the back. Oh, yes, one of them talked funny, like maybe he was a foreigner."

"Foreigner, huh?" I said half-aloud. Stella had grabbed me tonight, her husband was supposed to be working.... Barby had made a point of sitting at a table he served.... I forced the ugly thought aside. If Barby was knowingly in with the gang, why was she telling me this?

"When is all this supposed to happen?" I asked. "Their going to the police?"

"They couldn't agree on that. One kept saying that if they played it right, they could take care of you. That it might be playing right into your hands, that they didn't know anything about your real background. The lawyer seemed to think you might be some kind of special cop."

"The lawyer?" I asked sharply. "How do you know it was the lawyer that said that?"

"You said one of them was a lawyer." She colored slightly. "Anyway, the one that talked like maybe he had an education said that." She got up from the armchair, walked over and put her hands on my shoulders. "Am I being out of line, Toddy? Butting into something that I shouldn't?" She lay her head on my chest, snuggled close. Her hair tickled my nose.

"But you are curious?" I slipped my arms around her, pressed my hands on the small of her back. Her flesh was hot and soft beneath the shorty nightgown.

"I'm a woman," she whispered. "So it follows that I'm curious. I read that piece in the paper, and I said to myself: 'So that's what the big lug is up to. Gonna collect the money some crooked gamblers took away from grandmaw.' But I don't think it's funny, Darling.

"I know this town. I was born and raised here. We got some awful tough people here, as tough as they come. So I know you're piling up trouble for yourself.

"Why, Toddy? Do you think that the few dollars you can make this way is worth getting killed for, or maybe killing someone for? It's only money, Darling, you can live with it or without it." She stretched on tiptoe and kissed my chin, lightly. "I believe you when you say you didn't kill that girl on Tacoma Beach. I don't know if the police will, but if you stop going around looking for trouble, those men talked like they would love to forget all about going to the police." She shivered her body against me. "I know this sounds corny, and I know you won't like what I'm going to say, but I've got to say it.

"I've got money and this big old lonesome house—it's all yours if you want it." She buried her head under my chin, hugged me tight.

"What? A proposal, this early in the morning?" I lifted her by her bare hips, set her back from me. I let my eyes smile tenderly. "I didn't know you were interested in marriage, Beautiful."

"Marriage!" She wrinkled her nose. "I didn't say anything about marriage. Marriage is so-so final."

"Oh, you want me to be a kept man?"

"Damn!" she said crossly. "I want you alive and free. You're the first man I've met that I really like. You're a lot of fun and kicks. You think my way. We could have fun together. But you—you got to go around looking for trouble." Her green eyes suddenly twinkled. "I don't mind you having a good time. If your idea of a good time is to get into a fight, I'd like to have a ringside seat. I like to see a good fight, but—but I think you are picking on an organized gang of toughies, Darling. The odds are stacked against you."

"Maybe I like to play longshots?"

"It's something besides that," she said flatly. "Something's bothering you. I don't think that getting money back from crooked gamblers is all that you're after. I don't think that you really like to fight. If I may be so crude, what in hell is the matter with you?" She shot her underlip out at me. I'd seen the same look on spoiled six-year-olds.

"None of your damned business, Darling," I said with a laugh in my eyes. "You're made for milk and spice, and everything nice—not toughie roles. You take care of the homework and let me handle the wrecking business, huh? You wouldn't want to get mixed up with any murderers, would you?"

"I wouldn't want to get mixed up with a murderer, either," she said sharply.

"Then I'm in the wrong house. Sorry, Darling." I shoved her aside. "I really need some sleep. Thanks for the tip, but I've been expecting it. So thanks for nothing."

She stepped in front of me and grabbed my coat lapels, her green eyes shooting sparks.

"You big damn fool! I didn't mean you. Oh, hell, yes, I did, too. But you've got me all twisted up. So what you're doing is none of my damn business and I'm to keep my nose out. All right. All right," she said huskily. "But I only want to help."

"It's none of your fight," I said coldly. I took her hands from my coat, dropped them. "You're guessing pretty sharp, Baby. I've got something on my mind. Two somethings. One grew out of the other. Both of them are very unpleasant, both the result of crooked gambling. One of the two things is very personal. No one kills my last living relative and gets to go on living." I walked aimlessly around the high ceiling room, noticing the full length mirrors built into the walls. The carpeting with two inches of nap. The hand-carved wild cherry bedroom set.

"Anybody else live here with you?" I asked abruptly.

"No. Why?"

"Takes money—lots of money—for furniture, rugs and houses like this. Yours—or are you mooching off some sugar daddy?"

"You stupid, insulting sonofabitch," she said flatly. "Because a girl has some money, does she have to be rotten? Or does a girl have to be rotten to have money? Does the name Medina mean nothing to you?"

"Nothing," I answered shortly. "Right now something far more important is knocking around in my mind. I've been looking for some person that has control of gambling here in Newport. You make yourself available, you show me a good time, you warn me about something not even the police know about, offer me everything you can to stop my looking for this person. You live in a rich person's house, but have never dropped a hint about how you get your money. If you happen to be the person I'm looking for, you're only two steps away from hell!" "Toddy!" Her hand went to her lips, those green eyes opened wide, big in her suddenly small face.

"Toddy, you don't think I'd do anything to hurt you—?" She stopped, seeing the cold look of determination, the flatness of my eyes. She shuddered. "I don't know what you want," she said huskily. "I don't know what you're talking about. I'm sorry if my throwing myself at you made you think me cheap and common.

I thought we understood each other. I felt like we—like we sort of belonged. I guess I was wrong. You can go now." She wrapped her arms around her near nakedness, seated herself in the nearest chair. She sat very stiff, very straight, the only movement the jerking of a nerve in her lower lip.

I walked over to her slowly, watching her intently. She avoided my eyes with determination.

"I'm sorry," I said sincerely. "I'm acting like a goof because the pressure is building up around me. I've got the police watching me, I've got the whole gang of Newport hoodlums out after my skin. I know that someone is going to fix me for a murder rap. I've had very little sleep for two days and nights. But I've found the man who killed Kirk." She lifted startled eyes to mine. "Yes," I repeated softly. "I've found the man I came looking for. I'm trying to make up my mind: should I kill him and be satisfied—or should I let him wait until I get his boss, the one who gives the orders for death? What would you do, Beautiful?"

"Who is Kirk?" she blurted.

"A person who meant more to me than anybody in the world," I said bitterly. "While I was sitting in a hospital feeling sorry for myself, he sent me a letter asking me to come down here and buck this gambling crowd with him. I ignored it." I took a deep breath. "Then I got his funeral bill."

"I'm sorry," Barby said sympathetically.

"That doesn't help," I said harshly. "I asked you a question. Should I tear his murderer in little pieces now, or wait until I find the man—or woman—that ordered him to do it?"

"If someone killed a person I loved, I'd kill him if I could and the police didn't do it for me," she said slowly, twisting her hands together over her breasts. "I guess I would."

She untwisted her hands, grabbed me suddenly by the coat, pulled me to my knees in front of her.

ALFRED B. GLASER

"Oh, Darling, hold me!" Her voice was wild, trembling with emotion. "Hold me, Darling."

Her lips nuzzled my throat, she tilted her head back, ran her fingers up into my hair. Her mouth opened slackly, her lips dry from her heated breath. She unconsciously flicked her tongue over them, pulled my head down gently, placed her mouth on mine, moved her tongue with the darting intensity of sexy want. Her eyes stayed open, looking into mine, with the sunken, avid lustre of complete desire—and surrender. Her hot body was doing things to my hands, sending weakness ripping up my legs.

The bed was soft and smooth under my back. The pillow supported my head so that I could see the sun come charging up and gobble the weakened moon. Delicious waves of fatigue were sweeping over me. My eyelids weighted fifteen ton.

"Drink this, Darling."

I looked up slowly. Barby was bending over me, a glass in her hand, a soft smile on her lips. The rising sun made a rosy statue of her bare body. I took the glass.

"Brandy, Lover," she said, snuggling in beside me. "Guaranteed to make you sleep."

"I won't need that to sleep," I said, but took the glass, let the fiery liquid drain down my throat, send warm fire haloing out into my weary body. Drowsily I cupped one hand over the silky swelling part of her upper body, buried my face in the hollow of her throat and shoulder.

"I should have told you, Darling." Her voice sounded far away, lost in the rush of descending sleep. I felt one of her hands toying with my hair, felt the other one cover the one of mine that held onto her cool flesh, press it gently tighter. "About this house and me, I mean."

128

"Yes?" I asked from somewhere in dreamland, just before they closed the gates.

"Uh huh. You see, my mother and father died—that is, they were killed in a car wreck a couple of years ago—and they left me well off. Not too much, but enough to...." Her voice lost meaning, faded away.

CHAPTER NINETEEN

ARNDEST THING ... Rolling around in a rosebush. The thorns pricked my back, the smell of the roses sweet in my nostrils. Never felt thorns like that before—and no rose could be this big—no, it's a pillow. I lifted my head, turned it. Barby was rubbing my back, working her fingers into the muscles, kneading, soothing, stroking.

"Hey! I'm no hunk of dough to get ready for the oven," I yelped, squirming over on my side.

"I know a nicer way to wake you, but you might not approve." Barby wrinkled her nose at me and smiled. I reached up and got an armful, rolled her over onto the bed. Mussed her up a little, wrestled around a little, kissed a little, until we were finally gasping and clinging.

The hands of the clock pointed accusingly at nine-thirty. I tumbled out of bed, showered and rubbed down briskly. Dressed to the tantalizing smell of bacon and eggs frying. I followed my nose downstairs, through the big hall, pushed a door open. Barby, in a pink negligee, was bending over the stove, heavy iron griddle in her hand. From the look of the eggshells, she must have had a dozen spitting and popping on the griddle. The coffee aroma put a nice sharp edge to my appetite.

"Hi," she said. "Pour the coffee and sit. These'll be ready in a jiffy."

I poured the coffee, sat, watched Barby being domestic. Nice, but the negligee ruined it. A wife looking that desirable and lovely in the morning, cooking breakfast, was an impossibility. So I've been told—by many a despairing husband.

"If you had bobby pins in your hair—," I said with a grin in my eyes as she piled the eggs and bacon on my plate, "—and a patched morning robe on, instead of that peek-a-boo negligee and that soft, tawny, well-groomed hair, with those roses in your cheeks, this would be a swell domestic scene."

Barby smiled, put the rest of the eggs on her plate, put the griddle back on the stove, sat down. I already had a good mouthful of coffee down.

"I don't have a housecoat," Barby said. "All I did to my hair was brush it twelve times. As for the roses in my cheeks—a man's beard does that. Didn't you know?"

"Very becoming." I put my elbows on the table, bridged my hands, rested my chin. "Could run the rouge people out of business. Have to start a slogan: Beards better than rouge—rub a shine and save a dime."

"Eat," Barby commanded, jabbing her fork in the direction of my eggs. "A married woman has to put up with a poetic husband at the breakfast table. I don't."

"Bragging or complaining?"

"Not bragging, not complaining." She wrinkled her nose at me. "Just happy. Yesterday's gone, nothing I can do about it. Tomorrow's not here, so I can't do anything about that, either. But right now, this minute, I can. I'm eating, because I want to, I like to—and I need to."

"Also doing a lot of talking that you could have done yesterday or saved until tomorrow. I'm going to join your do-it-now club." I got up from the table. "I've got a feeling that maybe this morning my office phone will be ringing. I got a lot of free publicity last evening."

"You're not going to eat those eggs after I went to all the trouble?" Her eyes were sparking.

"Ah, ah! Making like a wife. Watch it!" But I didn't make the door. Barby slipped between the doorknob and my hand.

"So we'll forget the eggs," she said. "But isn't there something else?" She slipped her arms around my neck.

"Pucker up," I commanded sternly. I kissed her gently, firmly and absently. She nestled her head against my coat lapels, held tight.

"Mad about the eggs?" she asked timidly.

"Mad about you. But the daily grind must start."

"Something's the matter," she said, her voice muffled against my coat.

"Please?" I begged, trying to get the doorknob.

"No," she said, locking her arms tighter. "I want to know why you didn't touch a thing I fixed."

I tucked a finger under her chin, pried her face up. Damn if her eyes weren't damp.

"Got it bad, haven't you?" I asked gently. She slipped her chin free of my finger and buried her head again. "Look, Darling," I said awkwardly, "—there is a lot that you don't know about me. A lot I don't have time to tell you about right now."

"Why not?"

I thought it over. I wasn't being fair. Falling for a guy that couldn't eat breakfast with her. Tough, but I owed her an explanation.

"Okay. But I'll make it short. I have a—have a condition that would scare you out of your negligee if I started eating with you watching," I said stiffly.

"Is that why your face never moves? Why you talk with your lips slightly parted?" She leaned back, searched my face closely. She ran a finger lightly along a faint line. "Scar?" she asked.

"A surgeon's scar. There's quite a few."

"Why should that scare me?"

"If I move my face muscles, it will. I promise you. Please don't ask me to prove it." She saw the sincerity in my eyes.

"It wouldn't make a bit of difference," she said evenly. "When you know me better, you'll realize that. I think that your condition, whatever it is, is part of your being—being so vengeful. Right now, I don't want those eggs to go to waste." She led me back to the table, pushed me into the chair. "I won't watch. I'm going to run upstairs and get dressed. When I come back down, I want that plate clean."

"Little boy," I added for her wryly.

"Yes, little boy." She patted the top of my head and I heard her leave the kitchen, closing the door audibly.

The eggs were good. The second cup of coffee was good. I saw an open pack of cigarets on the drainboard and helped myself. The third cup of coffee tasted even better. I heard the door open, crashed the cigaret out in the plate.

"Feel better, Darling?"

I looked at her, stood up. What her body did to a simple dress was a pleasure. Her face was fresh, eager and happy, the lips slightly smiling.

"If I hadn't eaten so many eggs—," I said softly, "—I could butter you up and have an even better breakfast."

"Fried or roasted?" she asked impudently.

"You feel awful good roasting," I said wickedly. "I might take a chance on having you basted."

"Fresh," she retorted with a smile, her cheeks turning pink.

"What? Do I detect a blush?"

"Happiness lends the face color, Darling. I'm not ashamed of your wanting me. So there."

"Touché, but I've got to run. Can I give you a lift?"

"I have a car, Darling. I'm going for a long, slow drive. Spend the day dreaming. I'm going to make it a happy day. I've had so few," she ended with a touch of bitterness.

"Yesterday is gone, tomorrow is not here," I reminded her lightly.

"I hope—," she said wishfully, "—that you will be able to say that a week from now—about the yesterdays that are still the tomorrows."

Suddenly the smile and sparkle came back. She leaned forward, kissed me long and gentle, eyes open. She didn't touch me with her hands or body. We turned together and walked out into the sultry morning.

"My car's in the drive." She nodded her head at a late model sedan. "See you soon, Darling?"

"Soon," I promised.

I ducked behind the wheel of the 'Bird, keyed the motor to life. I waved to Barby standing on the walk, eased from the curb. I put Barby from my mind, concentrated on driving, left the words and impressions of the night before hang around the edge of my thinking. Out of it came one concrete fact: the gang was starting to split.

Barby had said that the four men couldn't agree on the frame. If Barby had overheard or had sat in on the supposed frame was beside the point; she had told me about it. If she was a member of the gang, she was coming over to my side. At least she didn't want me killed. Big John and his two pals had quit the city. Now Mule and Lefty were apparently arguing against the boss's decisions. Right at the time when the boss had to act fast, decisively and sure.

The boss's prestige couldn't stand anymore shoving around. If he did, the suckers would gain a cornered woman's courage and spit in his face—or hers.

I could expect the attack any moment. From the police or the gang. Or maybe both. If the police declared open house on me, the gang could grab guns and become good public spirited citizens, joining the deadly hunt.

I drove to the apartment, parked the 'Bird. Mike's Cadillac was gone. I went up and shaved, changed shirts and socks and underclothes. Had a glass of beer and a cigaret. By the time I decided to go to the office and not catch a quick snooze, it was twelve-thirty. As I went down to get the car, I hoped fervently I would have something waiting for me at the office that I could get my teeth into. Some squealer, some money hungry informer, anything that would give me a break, a chance to get to the boss before the boss unleashed his hounds of hell.

CHAPTER TWENTY

COULD HEAR THE PHONE RINGING as I unlocked the door to my office. I closed the door, picked up the phone in the reception room.

"Roscoe Todd," I said into the mouthpiece.

"Are you the man mentioned in the paper?" The voice was feminine.

"Yes, but how did you get my name and phone number?"

"I called the newspaper," the woman snapped impatiently. "They said that you might be able to say who the man was and gave me your number. Never mind that, I want you to beat the living daylights out of a two-bit chiseler for me. I'll pay a hundred dollars."

That damn reporter! The sly son had promised only not to print my name. He was probably glued to his phone, getting more information from these dumb suckers than I was—or would be. He could make them spill everything before he gave them the information they wanted. Most of the suckers wouldn't even stop to think that he was a newspaper reporter, someone they would never open their mouths to otherwise.

"Does it have anything to do with gambling?" I asked. It was a useless question. The reporter wasn't going to give my name and number to anyone unless it did. Of course, it would be a big help, him screening the applicants for me.

"It certainly does! This man won't let my husband alone. Always dragging him off somewhere for a game of cards. A friendly game, he says. Hrumpht! My husband always come back two or three hundred dollars short. Well, you want the hundred dollars?"

"Your name?"

"Rose Adams." She gave me her address. "It's an apartment. I'm on the second floor rear. You come here as soon as you can. I want to go with you when you get him."

From the sound of her voice, she wanted to kick him a few times after I knocked him down.

"I'll see you, Lady. But I'll have to have more information before I do anything."

"I'll give you all you want," she snapped.

"Until I see you, goodby." I cradled the phone, jotted the name and address on the phone pad.

Someone knocked on the door. The phone started ringing again. I went to the door, opened it.

"Come in," I said to the man standing there, walked over and picked the phone up.

"Roscoe Todd," I said, watching the nervous man rolling his brown hat in his hands. He was short and stocky, apparently a foreigner.

"Mr. Todd, I got your name from the newspaper. Could you tell me who the man is that is getting rough with the gamblers?"

"I'm the party you want."

"Then I want to talk to you. As soon as possible."

"Can't you tell me what it's about now? So I can judge how serious it is?"

"No. I won't discuss it over the phone."

"All right. What's your name and address?"

"Come to 413 Ft. Thomas Avenue. You don't have to know my name until you get here. Goodbye."

I put the phone down slowly, wrote the address on the scratch pad, turned to the man rolling the hat around in his hands.

"What can I do for you?" I asked.

"Mr. Todd? I'm Sperman—Nickolas Sperman. I run a restaurant," he said importantly.

"Yes?" Probably a greasy spoon hole in the wall.

"I called but couldn't get an answer, so I came personally." He looked the reception room over carefully, afraid there might be somebody hiding in a corner.

"What's your trouble?"

"It's my daughter. She's mixed up in something," he said uneasily.

"If it's about gambling, I'll listen." He nodded his head. "Come into my office."

I walked in with him following me. Before I got to the desk the phone was ringing. I let it ring.

Sperman couldn't tell me much. He wanted me to talk to his daughter, follow her if necessary. He was willing to pay. I finally promised to see his daughter, got rid of him. The phone was still wailing. A woman again. Sounded young and frantic. I got her name and address. After she hung up, I sat with the phone in my hand.

If the rush continued, I wouldn't have time to do any investigating. I needed help. I couldn't afford to miss any calls. The call you miss is always the one you didn't want to miss. I had to get some help right away.

I could call an employment agency. Probably get someone by the end of the week. Couldn't promise a steady job. No good. I thought of my time in the hospital, of the many men that would have jumped at the chance to earn a few extra dollars. The person I needed didn't have to be experienced. Just so they could answer the phone, take the message and write it down. I reached for the phonebook, opened it to the V's.

"Hello—Veterans's Administration?" The voice on the other end of the wire said yes. "I'm looking for someone to answer the phone and take messages. I don't care if they're man or woman, crippled or not. I'll pay sixty a week, but I don't know how long the job will last. Got anyone in mind?"

"I dunno. Quite a few guys wander in and out. I'll see what I can do."

"What about the hospital at Ft. Thomas? Will you try there for me?"

"Sure," the bored voice said.

I gave him my name and address, got his, remembered and gave him my phone number. In the next hour I picked up eleven names and addresses. Three persons were cranks. They wouldn't tell me how they got my name and number. One old cracked voice praised me for being a savior, promised to pray for me. He was real comforting, said that if I got killed to remember that Christ had also been killed for the good of mankind. I told him in a few words that my intentions had nothing to do with getting myself killed. He was disappointed.

Hunger was going to drive me from the office. My wristwatch had one forty-two. My stomach was saying that it needed something on top of those eggs. I could go to my apartment and eat. No one could get my phone number there, even if they tried. Not even the damn reporter. And two of the persons that called in sounded definitely like they had something to offer. That woman in Ft. Thomas, by her very evident cautiousness, probably knew a lot, going by the rule that a person who knows nothing talks a lot. I had to get out of the office. Time was running out. You can't start a steam roller and then stand in front of it forever. Sometime soon you had to get in the driver's seat—or get crushed. I heard someone come into the reception room, knock at my door.

"Come in."

She came in. Maybe I should say 'it' came in: tall, skinny, with a long face, wide cheekbones, steel gray eyes, brown hair, streaked with gray, cut close to the head—a female crewcut, shoulders erect, back straight. Her shoulders had a peculiar dip as she closed the door and walked the few steps to my desk. I noticed one leg dragged slightly. She opened one of those hand-carved, hand-stitched leather pocketbooks that hang by a strap from the shoulder and pulled out a piece of folded paper. With one of her big knuckled hands she laid it on the desk.

"Yes?" I said, looking at the folded paper on my desk.

"You called the Veterans' Administration? Wanted someone to take messages for you? Offered sixty a week? I'm here, I'll take the job. When do I start to work?" she said crisply, efficiently.

"And what is this?" I picked up the folded paper.

"My discharge. You seemed to prefer a veteran."

"You? A veteran?" I started to ask what war, but decided against it. She might still be carrying a handgrenade.

She marched around the desk, pulled the skirt of the severely tailored suit—it was a suit, I guess; it looked like what the WAC's wore, only it was blue—high, close to her hip.

I saw a flash of plain brown panties—and something else. It startled me.

"The Philippines. It's made of stainless steel," she said crisply, letting the skirt fall. "I wanted you to know and satisfy your curiosity at the same time. Most men and all girls are curious. I hope it doesn't interfere with my getting the job?"

"No. No, not at all," I said, getting my breath. I unfolded the paper in my hand.

"1st. Lt. Sarah Loren, 301 Battalion, United States Marine Corp," I read aloud. "Home Defense Medal, Pacific Theater Medal, Bronze Star, Purple Heart, Good Conduct Medal." I paused, read the rest of myself: some teeth that had been fixed up, a record of the stainless steel leg, other miscellaneous information a discharge carried. I stood up, saluted.

"Captain Roscoe Todd, USMC. Glad to have you aboard, Lieutenant." I handed her the paper, let my eyes smile. "Two casualties of the same war. We should get along fine."

She took the discharge, folded it neatly, opened her leather shoulderbag, tucked it in. Closed the bag with a snap.

"That is the end of the war," she said ironically. "I'm finished with it, it's finished with me. I'll call you Mr. Todd, you call me Miss Loren. What are my duties?"

"Duties?" I asked softly.

She flushed slightly. "Sorry. A slip. But what do I do? All my training has been of a military nature, so if I use military words occasionally, please ignore it."

"Okay. If you'll take that chip off your shoulder. Relax. Pull up that chair." I pointed to the dusty one in the corner.

She walked over to it, her shoulder dipping with each step, brought it back to the desk. Looked at the dust, frowned. She opened her shoulder bag, got a big square khaki handkerchief out, wiped the chair, sat down, put the big handkerchief back in her bag.

"Now, Miss Loren, your job is to take messages, mostly by phone, but maybe some of them will be from people who drop by the office. I'm interested in gambling, so I want you to find out who the people are, as much as you can about their trouble, if they have money or not, get their address or where they can be reached. I want that information written down in memo form and to hell with the English so long as I can read it."

"You're interested in gambling?" she asked sharply. "You are an investigator from Washington?"

"No. And I'm not a lawyer, either. What I'm doing is legal now, but I might be in jail any time. In case I am, I want you to go right on working. Take care of the office bills and all that."

"You're no lawyer?" she frowned. "You work for nobody? How do you make any money?"

"I get ten percent of all the money I collect from gamblers that got it the crooked way," I said.

"But if you're not a lawyer—I mean, how can you collect it?"

"I have my ways," I said dryly. "But it won't get you in any trouble, legal or otherwise. To put it bluntly, I play rough, so you're free to leave anytime you want. But I don't think anyone would bother you."

"I can take care of myself," she said harshly. "I've been doing it for more years than I care to remember."

"It won't be necessary, I'm sure. But I'll be out of the office most of the time, so I'd like for you to be here at nine-thirty to five, with an hour out for lunch. Is that all right?"

"But suppose I have to get in touch with you?" she asked. "How am I supposed to do it?"

"You don't, I guess. You'll have to wait until I call in or come in."

"If you would give me your home number, I could call you in the morning if you didn't get here."

"Forget it. Nothing will be that important." I looked at her closely. "Miss Loren, would you mind if I called the V. A. and checked with them?" The thought had suddenly occurred to me that this would be a wonderful way to keep tabs on me—and to shut the blabbermouths wailing at my office door.

"Please do," she said shortly. "I want you to be sure that I'm not a crooked gambler."

"I'm sorry," I said. "But I've got to watch all ends. Do you happen to have their phone number?"

"As much as I've haunted the place for a job, I should have," she said bitterly, reaching for the phone and dialing. She handed the receiver to me.

"I'm Mr. Todd," I said when I heard the receiver lifted. "Are you the person I talked to about getting someone to take messages?"

"Yeah. Did she show up?" the bored voice said, annoyed. "Mister, don't blame me. You said anyone. She happened to drop by, so I unloaded her on you."

"Thanks," I said dryly. "Have you known her long?"

"Too long," the annoyed voice said. "That crabby old maid has had more jobs than a latrine orderly. Don't knock the chip off her shoulder or she'll cuss you out for being un-American. All that stuff about fighting the war and not being appreciated—you probably know the type."

"Yeah," I said slowly. "Been one of them myself, you chair-warming buzzard." I slammed the receiver down.

"Nice people, these boys who look after our welfare, aren't they?" she said laconically.

"Yeah. Oh, I'm sorry, Miss Loren, but have you had lunch?"

"Yes. Thank you."

"I haven't," I said, getting up. "The place is all yours. I'll be back when you see me. By the way, here's a key." I fished in my desk drawer until I found the spare. "If you need any supplies or anything, use this as petty cash." I handed her a fifty-dollar bill. "Hold the fort, Lady Marine."

"Consider it held, *MR*. Todd," she said, taking the bill. "And please try to forget I was a Lady Marine."

The phone rang as I went out the door. The action a front page write-up can bring, I thought wryly. After two months digging with nothing happening, I get a little write-up in a newspaper and wham, everybody wants to cry on my shoulder. But that's what I wanted, so what was I getting growly about?

After a thick steak and some dry wine, I decided I wasn't getting growly—I was only hungry. But I had my work cut out for me. I hated to interview all those people who called, but I had to. Hard work. Slow work. And I didn't have much time. While I was out questioning some surly woman whose equally surly husband had lost the rent money, something hot could come in on the phone at the office. I was hoping that some member of the gang had stumbled on to who the boss was and would be able to spill it for enough money. That was the only chance I had, up to now. Sheila had said her price was to get out of the gang. It it was true or not, the important thing was—she did have a price. She had made the first positive identification of any member of the gang. That was an important bit of help. Newport swarmed with gambling men, but a small percent were organized. Until then, I had no way of telling who was a gang member.

I couldn't very well call the office every five minutes. The office had no way of calling me.... or did it? Of course! The local call service. Doctors used it. Real estate men. I called the waitress over, asked her for a phone book.

It took a little hunting, because I didn't know how it was listed. I found the service, copied the address, paid my bill and went out and stooped into the 'Bird.

It took about twenty minutes, plus a sizeable hunk of money to get immediate service. But I stood on the sidewalk with a small plastic box in my hand, perforations in the shape of a star on the front, a button on the side. If I let the button on all the time, the batteries would last thirty-six hours—and I could get short messages any time of the day or night. That was what I was paying for, so I let the button rest on the 'on' mark, put it in my left jacket pocket, the one by the shoulder where a fancy hanky is supposed to go.

I went to the nearest street phone booth, dialed the number the call service had given me.

"Call Service. Your message, please?" The voice was impersonal, brisk.

"Tell Mr. Todd to contact his office, please."

"Just a moment." I heard the impersonal voice ask somebody something. Probably didn't have my name registered to the girl on the switchboard.... heard some paper rustling. "We will contact Mr. Todd. The message is: Mr. Todd to contact his office. Thank you." I heard the plug pulled.

A tiny, ghostly voice started paging me from my coat pocket.

"Mr. Todd, call your office. Mr. Todd, call your office. Mr. Todd, call your office." Three times the tiny voice urged me to call my office. I found myself automatically dialing my office, listened impatiently to the busy signal. Realized what I had done, shook my head wryly.

I pressed the handle down on the phone, waited a minute, tried again. Might as well tell Miss Loren about it—might do a little checking while I was at it. This time I got an answer.

"Mr. Todd's office." Miss Loren's voice came crisply over the wire. "What can I do for you?"

"If Mr. Todd is out, your confidence will be respected. Would you care to leave a message? If your troubles are about gambling, please tell me as much as you want to, and if Mr. Todd thinks it's serious enough, you leave your name and address and he will contact you."

"I'm afraid," I whispered back.

"Nonsense," Miss Loren said distinctly. "You have absolutely nothing to be afraid of. Once Mr. Todd's services are sought, your troubles are over. Now please tell me what's bothering you, and if you are in any danger, come directly to this office."

I placed the receiver gently on the hook. Let her puzzle over that one. The phone jangled noisily. I looked at it. After all, it was a public phone. I shrugged, answered it.

"I'm sorry you were cut off," the operator said. "Here is your party."

"Please give me the number in case we are cut off again," I heard Miss Loren request.

"I'm sorry," I said contritely. But I really called to tell Your party is on the line."

"Good try," I said. "But you'll find it is almost impossible to get a phone number from an operator."

"Who is this?" Her voice was sharp, insistent.

"Don't blow a fuse," I said lightly. "This is your boss man testing. Congratulations, you're doing fine."

"Mr. Todd, really!" There was a hint of anger in that efficient voice.

"I'm sorry," I said contritely. "But I really called to tell you that I have subscribed to the call service." I gave her the number. "If you have anything you think I might want to know, call that number and they will contact me."

"I will. But are you coming in? I have a few messages for you, but they are all call-backs. I could give you the numbers and you can call them."

"Not now. I'm going out to see a party. When I get back, I'll check some of those calls."

"Where are you going? I have a call here from a lady in Ft. Thomas. She said she called you earlier, but that she was afraid you might not be interested because she didn't give her name— only her address—and wouldn't tell you why she wanted to see you. She said that if you called her, she would tell you more about it. I thought maybe if you were going out that way, you could stop by."

"That's odd," I said thoughtfully. "I was thinking of calling on that lady anyway, I think. Is the address 413 Ft. Thomas Avenue?"

"Yes, and her name is Mrs. Leeds. If anything comes up, can I contact you there?"

"Use the call service, Miss Loren," I said. "I'm paying good money for its use, and that way you can be sure I'll call you right back. Bye now." I put the phone on the hook. Mrs. Leeds, huh? Now I knew the name of the party I was going to talk to, anyway. I'd had a hunch about that call before.... better not get too excited, probably just another Mrs. Ruhle.

Barby had been in the back of my mind most of the day. As I drove towards Ft. Thomas, I brought my thoughts concerning her out into the open.

That she was connected with the gang, I was pretty sure. Probably got in with them for the kicks. How deep she was in was what bothered me. Had she actually sat in on the discussion that was supposed to have taken place in the Frontier Bar? Oh had she been just hanging around, killing time while the four talked. In short, was she a 'hanger-on', a fellow traveler, or did she actually take part in the gang's operations? If she was a part of it, a big part of it, and was playing me for a sucker.... I hated to think of that. But she did try to help me. True, she was using the threat as a lever to get me to quit my meddling, just like Stella used the promise of her available body to sidetrack my interest.

Could I help it if Barby had drifted, had mingled with the wrong crowd? Would she help me if the chips were down? I decided to give her the chance. Whatever information she gave me I could weigh against the knowledge that she did belong to the gang before I used it. But if she was in deep, she could lead me into a horrible trap. I pushed the thought back, slammed on the brakes in front of one of those glassed-in phone booths.

I went into the hot cubicle and dialed Barby's number. She might be back from her drive.... she was.

"Hello, Soul-shaker," I said. "Your current boy friend."

"Toddy!" Barby said, a nice sound in her voice. "Want to come and share a cold beer with me?"

"Sorry, Honey. Got work to do. But I'd like to ask a favor?"

"Of course, Lover. Want me to shoot somebody?"

"Gosh, no. But I forgot to thank you for telling me about what you heard the other night. I want you to know I appreciate it."

"Want me to do some snooping, huh?"

"You're sharp, Sweetheart. Not snooping. Just keep your pretty eye open and your ear to the ground. Some chance word you might hear could help a lot."

"Of course, Darling. I'm going to put on same glad rags and start making the rounds of the gambling dives."

"Better be careful. You told me how tough these local boys are, remember?"

"Pooh!" she said, laughing. "Barby is just a not so big dumb blond. Besides, I've been around most of those dives some time or other."

Sheila with a broken neck came to my mind. Cold fingers played on my back.

"Honey, please don't do anything silly. I mean it. This gang plays for keeps."

"So?" she said harshly. "Maybe it'll help if you have to worry a little about me. My worrying about you has been a little one-sided, it'll help to have company. Please, Darling, why don't you drop it? I do know how rough these bums can play—I've lived here all my life, as you just said."

"Too late," I said shortly. "But if you do stick that lovely neck out, at least keep in touch with me." I gave her my call number, told her how it worked. "You will call me once in a while? Let me know where you are?"

"Of course, Darling. Gee, that call service is nice. All I have to do is ring your number and say 'Come to the Frontier Bar, quick,' and I got myself a date. I'm going to have all my boy friends start carrying one of those things."

"Please be serious, Barby."

"All right, Toddy. "I'll be careful. You be careful, too. If you need me, holler. If they get after you, you can always hide under my bed."

"Under your bed?" I asked softly.

"I'll get under it with you," she giggled.

"Take it easy, Honey," I said. "I'll see you tonight at one of the dives. Bye now."

"Bye. I'll let you know what dive I'm in—I don't want you to waste too much time hunting for me."

CHAPTER TWENTY-ONE

I LEFT THE PHONE BOOTH, revved the 'Bird up, and aside from getting lost twice, finally parked it in front of 413 Ft. Thomas Avenue. I got out into the broiling four o'clock sun and walked up to the large house, thankful for the shade trees that surrounded it. I used the brass knocker and pounded on the door. A young colored maid answered.

"Is Mrs. Leeds in?" I asked.

"Who should I say it is that's calling?" she asked impudently.

"Mr. Todd."

"Just a minute." She closed the door firmly in my face, opened it a half-minute later. "You come on in, Mrs. Leeds will see you."

I went in, noticed the maid hook a heavy steel chain back into a slot on the door, followed her across the dark paneled reception hall, waited while she opened a sliding door.

"Mr. Todd to see you, Ma'am."

"Show the gentleman in." The voice was old and testy. I stepped in, smelling lavender as I passed the maid.

Mrs. Leeds was seated in an antique chair. One of those kind with an impossible straight back. Her hair was silver gray and wispy, framing a face of parchment skin and coarse bones, with bright shoe-button eyes. She had knitting going in her dry, wrinkled hands, the needles flashing in the shaft of sun stealing by the thick brocaded curtains. Those shoe-button eyes watched me without blinking.

"I want you to do something about my daughter," she said hoarsely. "She's got herself mixed up in a rotten bunch. They'll make a bitch out of her if she keeps playing with them."

"Ma'am!" I said reprovingly.

"Bosh! A bitch is a female hound dog. Perfectly good word. In every dictionary. They print worse words in the newspaper today. So don't 'Ma'am' me. If I say she'll be a bitch, she'll be a bitch." She reached into the knitting basket, got an envelope. "Here, take this. It ought to be enough for your troubles."

"Now wait a minute," I snapped. "If it has anything to do with crooked gambling, I'll look into it. If not, I'm not interested."

"Of course it has to do with crooked gambling." She leaned forward and shoved the envelope in my hands. Her breath smelled of stale beer. "There's a thousand dollars there, you won't have to count it. Now you go knock some sense in that daughter's head. You'll find her in one of those fancy houses on Orchard Road. Sixty-nine is the number."

"What's her name? And I want information—not knock sense into someone's head," I rasped. The old harridan was getting on my nerves.

"Mrs. Lawton. She's married to a no good punk. Now get out."

I turned on my heel, stalked out of the room. The maid opened the door with a mocking smirk on her lips. I stopped on the walk under the shade trees, put the envelope into my inside coat pocket. The sense of being trapped grew by the minute. I couldn't shake it.

Impatiently I walked out into the blazing sun and jack-knifed into the 'Bird. I started the motor and got the car rolling in the thick, heated air.

Number 69 Orchard Road was hard to find. After talking to a jerk in a filling station, who steered me wrong, I drove around until I found it. The house was in need of repair, the paint peeling from the clapboard sides. I didn't like the idea of it being the last house on the rutted lane that passed for Orchard Road. I didn't like it any better than I had liked the smell of stale beer on the old harridan's breath.

I was ready for anything when I knocked on the open door, shoved it all the way open and stepped in when no one answered. Even ready for the twin eyes of the double-barreled shotgun that lined up on my belly.

The man holding it, like any punk, wasn't ready to pull the triggers. He needed that split second it takes to screw up his kind of killing courage.

That split second gave me time to duck, place the palm of my hand on the twin barrels and ram the shotgun and its owner across the dusty room. The double load of buckshot tore a hole in the ceiling, showering plaster down. I grabbed the hot barrel, clubbed the stock across the punk's shoulder blades, saw the stock split when it mashed into the broken shoulder blades as far as it could go.

"You got the bastard!" The hoarse cry came from the next room. "Told you the dumb sonofabitch would walk right into those buckshot!"

The owner of the hoarse voice walked right through the door into my balled right first. He spun around limply, not even knowing what hit him. I controlled a horrible impulse to splatter his brains on the dusty floor with the barrel of the shotgun. I compromised by hurling the broken end of the stock into his upturned face.

I went into the room he had come out of, saw the whiskey bottle and greasy cards on the table, the two punks' coats draped on the chair-backs. I walked to the back door, looked at the flashy two-toned car parked there. Then I walked swiftly back through the two rooms, kicking shattered plaster with my shoes, shut the front door after me. I sprinted for the 'Bird, twisted it to life, slewed it around on the rutted lane and kicked dust getting away from there.

"The damn clever murdering boss!" I ground it out between locked teeth as I swung the 'Bird onto Alexander Pike. "Using the newspaper article to lead me to a death trap! How many of those other calls are death traps? The clever murdering sonofabitch!"

"Talking to yourself, Roscoe," I said to myself aloud, still talking to myself above the rush of wind created by the speeding 'Bird. "They put you in straitjackets, strapped you down and got the fire hose ready when you started talking to yourself in the hospital. Knew that you were losing control—now cool down, take it easy. Quit your babbling."

I locked the brakes and burned forty foot of rubber coming to a stop in front of 413 Ft. Thomas Avenue. Leaving the motor running, I vaulted out of the 'Bird and made the front door of the house in ten bounds. I almost splintered the door when I knocked on it.

"Calm down!" I told myself aloud savagely. "You got work to do. Don't undo it all by losing control of yourself now!"

I heard the bolt being drawn on the door. It opened a crack. One frightened eye of the maid looked out at me over the loop of the steel safety chain. I slammed the heel of my hand into the door and pushed. The two inches of slack in the steel chain saved the maid from being murdered by the door edge. The chain stopped most of the savage drive from my arm before it snapped, the slowed door spilling the maid onto the hall floor. She scrambled on all fours for the safety of the stairs, bleating like a stuck pig.

When I burst in on the old harridan, she still had the quart bottle of beer of beer suspended between mouth and table. I slapped it out of her startled hand.

"You murdering old bitch!" I rasped, taking a handful of her dress over her skinny chest, lifting her out of the chair. "Who in hell gave you the orders to send me into that death trap? Talk, damn you, before I slap your filthy face into bloody pulp."

"Ha, ha, ha—hah!" she cackled drunkenly into my blazing eyes. "I knew the two-bit whore-hoppers from Brooklyn would bungle the job! I told that gutter-snipe Mule so! If he'd let me do what I wanted to, I'd of picked a horse pistol out of my knitting basket and blasted you to hell when you walked into the room before! Gotta be fancy—all these bums gotta be fancy!" She grinned evilly at me.

I slapped her, palm of hand and back of hand, dropped her onto the antique chair. She lost her balance and toppled drunkenly onto the floor. She lay there and looked up at me with blazing eyes.

"You got no call to do that!" she screeched, one clawed hand rubbing her cheek. "I'll have the police on you for that!"

"Then call them, damn you!" I said savagely. "Get up from your stinking behind and call them!"

She scrambled crab-like for the little round stool that held the phone. The damn fool really meant to call the police! Hell, she had a perfect right to! What cop would believe a wild story like mine? In a couple of hours—after they checked 69 Orchard Lane—they might. If the two punks were still there.

I stepped over her and ripped the phone wires loose, kicked the small round stool across the floor.

"You murdering old bitch," I said disgustedly. "I ought to kick your brains out. Since you told me who brained the frame, I'll let your drunken old hide alone." I spun on my heel, headed for the door. "You give me any reason to come for you again, have a pine box ready for your smelly carcass."

"You won't get far, you whore-hopping maniac!" she screeched. "You wait and see who's going to need the pine box!"

I stalked through the reception hall and out the door with the threat ringing in my ears, gunned the 'Bird to life and headed for Newport, my blood still boiling, my mind in a turmoil.

It was hopeless. I wasn't going to get to the boss. Then to hell with the boss. Get Mule, get the guy that killed Kirk and Sheila. That much I could do. That was why I was here, in this hot, stinking, corrupted town. So why not do and have it done with? Why not?

Was it because somewhere along the trail I had found that my face and personality would and did fit into society? That I wasn't a complete freak? That I wanted to hunt, and fish, and relax with a cold bottle of beer, to watch the summer turn to autumn, to winter, to spring. Hear the snow crunching under my shoes, to feel free rain in my face, to argue presidents with my elbows hooked over a bar. Watch the pasteboards fall and the horses run. Hold a girl in my arms—I wanted to live again, after all those long years.

But I knew I couldn't. Not while Kirk's murderer walked and watched and played on the same green earth. Not while half of me ached and felt lonely, dead. Not while a happy but puzzled face looked at me in my dreams.

I swung the 'Bird over onto the shoulder of the road and buried my head in my folded arms on the steering-wheel. I let myself sink into misery and regret, rooted around in self pity and contempt, with cars swooshing by, tires singing on the pavement, hot air eddying in the stuffy heat. Loneliness can be an aching, eating hell.

I pulled my head from my folded arms, sat back against the cushions, holding onto the steering-wheel with both out-stretched arms, eyes staring vacantly into space. The savage, boiling fury was stirring in me again. The urge to have and be done with it sweeping over me, to tear and rend and mash into a bloody pulp the living body of Adam Coasta—Mule.

I knew what was the matter with me, sitting here gripping the steering wheel with white, clenched hands. I didn't need a headshrinker to tell me. My mind was teetering on the edge of a murdering mania, and I was through trying to control it.

I mashed the gas pedal to the floor, jumping the 'Bird into the swooshing traffic with screaming rubber. A coldness, a calmness had me, but heat lightning was flickering in my vitals, singing and snapping in my brain. If this is what it's like to be crazy, I thought icily, then lunacy is the last outlet for people with their backs to the immovable wall, and the jump into oblivion is a welcome finality.

I'm really crazy, I thought, as I shot under the rail-road bridge coming into Newport on Monouth Street, I'm hearing voices already. Tiny, ghostlike voices!

"Mr. Todd. Urgent. Barby says run. Mr. Todd. Urgent. Barby says run. Mr. Todd. Urgent. Barby says run." The ghost voice stopped. The voice seeped into my ears, dug tiny fingers into my brain. I came back to the present with an icy suddenness.

"What the devil?" I muttered to myself. "Barby says run? The call service!"

I slammed on the brakes and nosed the 'Bird into the curb, across from a glassed-in phone booth. I let the motor run, dodge the one-way traffic. Went into the phone booth, pulling Barby's phone number from my mind, digging in my pocket for change. Across the street a police cruiser braked to a stop by the 'Bird. I lifted the receiver—helluva time to get a ticket, I thought—then I dropped the receiver.

Two policemen were climbing warily out of the cruiser with short, wicked riot guns held ready.

CHAPTER TWENTY-TWO

WATCHED THE POLICE WITH UNWILLING FASCINATION. One of them stayed by the cruiser, his sawed off automatic shot gun hung in the crook of his elbow. With his free hand he reached into the cruiser, feeling blind with the hand, his eyes flicking along the crowded street.

He pulled the little mike out, spoke into it. The second officer walked around the 'Bird, the riot gun held at port, setting his feet down as though he was walking on eggs. He completed his circle, came back to the officer with the mike in his hand.

They stood tense, looking slowly along the street on the side the 'Bird was parked on. In seconds their close, slow scrutiny would swing to this side. And I was standing in a glass telephone booth, not twenty feet from them.

Barby had said run. I backed warily out of the booth. Sidled into the five o'clock crowd, mixed with them. I almost made it, would have if the police had not double parked their cruiser.

It was blocking a line of traffic and the drivers had seen the riot guns. Some of the citizens on the sidewalk had also noticed. I made the mistake anyone is apt to make under the circumstances. I was unconsciously sneaking among the people, watching the police at the same time. I bumped a lady with bundles. One of the drivers in the stalled cars had noticed me.

"Hey, Officer!" I heard him yell. "There's a big guy on the other side of the street acting like he's trying to duck. Over there!"

I started running, ducking around suddenly excited and agitated people.

"Halt!" I heard the officer shout.

No police officer is going to open up with a riot gun on a crowded street. They could get me if they could run faster. I ran down Monouth Street, towards Ninth. If I could make the next square, the crowds were thicker. There I could offer less of a target, be shielded better by the crowds. My one chance was ducking into a big store, abruptly acting normal. Big stores had back doors, basements, roofs.

I made the crossing on Ninth, dodging cars. The crowded street was aware of something unusual. Sirens opened up from other parts of the city, their banshee wail growing loud. Shouting was breaking out behind as the crowd hysteria swept down the street after me. A big department store was three doors away.

"Wow!" I said in a voice that carried, as I walked casually in the door. "The cops sure are having a big time out there! Got somebody on the run. Chasing him with sawed-off shotguns. Don't get on the street!" I yelled at a lady starting out the door. "Those cops might start shooting!"

She stopped dead, her eyes rolling like a calf's. Immediately everybody that heard the yell started for the door, jamming, standing on tiptoe, craning their rubber necks, babbling excitedly. By now the sirens were loud and clear, some of them burbling down and whining out.

I moved casually back through the store, sending the curious customers heading for the front with the same rapid explanation. Some of the clerks forgot their counters and joined the mob jammed up front.

The back of the store had a balcony stuck close to the ceiling, where those little money-changers on wires duck into. Under the balcony were more counters. I couldn't see any doors opened out back. I had to chance the stairs up to the balcony.

I got up the stairs without anyone noticing, opened the door at the top and walked into an office with six desks. Two girls were busy at work handling the wire cages. I walked over to a young girl with heavy glasses, busy stuffing papers in a filing cabinet.

"Pardon me," I said. "Could you tell me the way to the next floor?"

"What?" she asked in a voice as vague as her eyes.

"I said, is there a way up to the next floor? You know, upstairs?"

"I don't know what you want," she said absently, frowning at a paper she pulled from the filing cabinet. "See Mr. Stacy over there."

A commotion broke out down below. I looked toward the front of the store in time to see police ramming their way through the crowd at the door, riot guns held high. A chill went down my spine. Two of the police had rifles. The way they handled them coming through the crowd showed they knew how to use them. A man got up from a desk on one side of the office at the sound of the commotion, gave me a startled glance, went quickly over to the balustrade.

"What's going on down there?" he shouted.

The police stopped pouring down the aisles between the counters, and looked up. I felt their eyes bore into me.

"Get down!" one of them yelled. "Get down on the floor. Quick! That's a maniac standing behind you!"

The man on the balustrade gripped the rail hard, swayed. He turned frightened eyes on me, his mouth working, no sound coming out. The girls froze at their work.

"Down! Get down, you crazy fools," an officer yelled from the floor. "That man takes a notion he'll tear you apart before we can get to you!"

The officer snapped his rifle to his shoulder. I ducked, swung on my heel the same instant the rifle cracked. I heard the slug snap as it went by my head, then splat as it buried itself in the wall. Everybody on the balcony clawed their way down on their bellies, two girls trying to get under the same desk.

Another rifle cracked. I felt a hot streak across my neck, just below my ear. I dove headlong for one of the windows, slid up against the wall.

"You got him!" one of the girls screamed frantically. Then as I came to my knees, grabbed the bottom of the window, she screamed again. "No! No, you didn't get him. Hurry. Oh, please hurry!"

I put savage strength into a yank upwards on the window hooks. The window opened easily, shot up. As I slid over the sill, it hit the top with a crash and glass showered down on me, fell with me to the alley below. Tinkled around me as my knees bent under the impact, pitched me forward. I rolled, came onto my feet, half fell over a stack of garbage cans and ducked between two buildings onto a narrow walk.

I sprinted, came out on York Street. I went across York Street in one falling lunge, over an iron picket fence, into someone's front yard, between the houses, jumping a back fence into an alley. Pounding down the alley to Eighth Street, I turned right and walked hastily back to York Street, joined the crowd. Everywhere I looked, I saw police.

A cruiser was parked twenty feet from me, nosed into the curb, motor still running, no one in it. Citizens were craning their necks, looking down York Street, talking excitedly.

All the police were concentrating on York Street, where I had crossed before. They broke apart, two of them sprinting up towards me, dodged around the corner and went pounding down Eighth Street. If they had looked across Eighth, they would have seen me edging over to the police cruiser.

I hoped the police were still putting on a good show as I opened the door of the cruiser, slipped back of the front seat, closed the door softly. I hunched down on the floorboards, wedged myself tight against the back of the driver's seat. Lying on the back seat was an emergency blanket, one of those kinds some cruisers carry to throw over accident victims. I pulled it off the seat and draped it carefully over me. I huddled there and listened to the police radio squawk.

It was as hot as hades under the blanket. I felt blood from my neck trickling down my chest. For awhile I was safe. If the police came back to the cruiser and checked it, I was a gone duck. But the odds were against it. Regardless, I had no choice. I had to play the cards as they dropped, make any plans for a minute at a time. To plan further ahead right now might be useless. I heard the beat of hurrying feet, the door of the cruiser was jerked open on the driver's side, somebody climbed in, the door slammed. I heard a click as the radio was switched from receiving to sending.

"Car Eleven. Car Eleven. Proceeding down Eighth, will cruise Isabelle." The mike switch clicked, the radio came on.

"Car Eleven, proceed as stated. Proceed as stated. Wait further instructions. That is all."

The cruiser backed up from the curb, went forward, made a turn. What a cop, I thought, going the wrong way on a one-way street. Hope he doesn't wreck the cruiser. He turned, stopped.

"See anything of him?" the officer in the cruiser asked.

"Beats me where he got to." The right front door opened, the car sagged as another officer got in. "We're supposed to cruise Isabelle?"

"Yeah. The other cruisers are covering the streets down to the Licking River. I don't see how he can get away," the driver said, started the car to moving.

"He's a tough cookie. Hope he doesn't get the jump on anybody. He'd kill them sure as hell. That girl in the store said he's hit bad, said Steve knocked him down with that rifle bullet."

"I dunno," the driver said. "Those gals were almost as scared as that manager. All of them probably had to change pants. Take it from me, he's probably over in Covington by now. He's had enough time to get to the river and swim across. Tom and Eddie—they were the ones that spotted him—said he can outrun a deer. Me, I hope I don't bump into him. I got a wife and kid."

"Aw, hell, Al. You with that riot gun and me with this .03? What chance would he have? We could blast him to hell before he blinked an eye."

"Yeah. But what if he steps out in your face? He'd probably tie them around our necks. Old Hogie said in the briefing that he has more strength in his one hand than we have in our whole body. No siree, if I see him and he's as close as ten feet, I'm running."

"Hell, what good would that do you?" the partner snorted. "Tom and Eddie said he could outrun a deer. You with that fat gut wouldn't have a chance."

"I don't think he wants to chase any of us police. I'd take a chance on that, anyway. Sure don't aim to jump him unless I have to," Al said. "Hey! The radio. Listen."

I couldn't hear what the message was. It was muffled and not clear.

"Car Eleven. Car Eleven. Not a sign. Everything quiet." Silence, except for the hum of traffic on the street.

"Like I said, he's probably over in Covington by now," the officer on the right said with a sigh. "Just as well sit back and relax. Might give out a few tickets. The old man in traffic was hotter than hell about seeing ten overtime parkers on Monouth Street without tickets the other day."

I felt the officer on the right squirm around in the seat, something plopped by me on the back seat.

"Here, Al, give me that riot gun. No use hugging that thing and driving, too."

"Don't throw it back there the way you did the rifle. Blow us to hell."

"Okay, okay." I heard the other gun go on the seat, make a slight snicking noise as it bumped the rifle.

"Hey, you're getting damn careless with that blanket! Got it all over the back of the car, Al. Old Man sees that, he'll chew us both out."

"Huh?" Al said.

"I said the blankets all over the back of—" That was as far as he got. He choked on the rest.

I snaked one hand out from under the blanket, grabbed the riot gun. I stayed on the floor, but the muzzle of the riot gun was looking in Al's partner's face.

"Easy does it!" I said softly. "Like you said, I don't want to kill any policeman. Drive real careful and tell your partner to stick his eyes back in. Don't try to be a hero and all of us might five. As you know, I don't have a thing to lose."

The cruiser wobbled slightly, straightened. They sat in frozen silence. I watched the sweat trickle down from under their uniform caps.

"Go on talking, acting natural. If you have to stop, don't either of you get out of the car unless you have to. If one of you do get out of the car, and make the slightest wrong move, you will kill your partner as sure as if you pulled the trigger."

"What do you expect to gain?" Al asked in a dry, stiff voice.

"A chance. Just a chance to get away for a little while," I said with a deadly quiet. "I have a score to settle. Then I might walk into the police station and give myself up."

"Now, look," the one on the right said, fighting to keep his voice calm. "Let us drive you to the station. You won't get hurt. That way there'll be no shooting, you'll get a fair trial."

"Thanks. I appreciate that," I said dryly. "But I've got a killing to do. If I have to kill both of you to get the job done, then I have to kill you. Sorry."

"You've done enough killing," Al said sharply.

"Sorry, Al. I haven't killed anyone. Not yet. Who did I supposedly kill?"

"Two men saw you kill that girl out at Tacoma. After they signed the statement, you got to one of them. But the one left is enough to fry you," Al said harshly.

"I didn't kill Sheila Thomson." I wasn't going to argue with them. "Who is the other one that I'm supposed to have 'stopped'?"

"Didn't kill Murdock, either?" Al asked sarcastically.

"Lefty?" I asked, surprised.

"Yeah. Lefty Murdock. Don't know anything about it, huh?"

"When did this happen?"

"Few hours ago," Al snorted. "Busted all to hell in his apartment, as if you didn't know. Guess you want to get the other one, too."

No wonder that old harridan, Mrs. Leeds, was so anxious to call the police. She probably knew the frame had been put in motion. If those two punks had killed me, it wouldn't have changed anything. That was extra insurance the boss had bought. Besides keeping me out of town with no alibi for Lefty's murder, there was a good chance that my mouth would be closed for good. They would have dumped my body in some convenient place for the police to find and that would be that. The book on

Sheila's and Lefty's murder would be closed and placed on the dusty shelf with Kirk's.

" I want you to drive this cruiser to some nice secluded spot, and I mean secluded. No tricks. I'm tired of your company," I said shortly. "Do as I say, and you can tell your grandchildren all about the maniac you rode around with. Try any tricks and your grandchildren will get it from the newspapers.

"When you stop this car there, I'm going to peep out, the safety catch off this riot gun. If it's a trick, we'll all go to hell together."

"So you got yourself a taxi," Al said. "We take you to a secluded spot, then what? You bump us, hull?"

"You have a choice, maybe?"

"Yeah. We can get ourselves bumped right here. Then we know you go with us."

"You want to die? What about that wife and those children you mentioned awhile ago? If I wanted to kill you, I could have done it already. You might be parked in front of the police station right now, for all I know. Or are you hoping that someone in a passing bus or truck will notice this shotgun pointed up the seatback at your head?

"Every second you hesitate brings you closer to a load of buckshot. I'll number those seconds for you. I'll give you ten more, then either start driving or go for your pistols, but remember your brains won't look good splattered on a busted windshield.

"I've finished talking. I'm starting to count. One—"

"What's the word, Al?" his partner asked in a jerky voice.

"I'm not ready to die," Al said in a dry, cracked voice. "We don't have a prayer this way. If we drive him where he wants to go, we might get a chance. It's better than—this."

"Anything is better than this," Al conceded. "Where to, you crazy bastard?"

"You pick the place," I said dryly. "Just remember if anyone sees us—boom."

"Let's take him over where they park all those brewery trucks. We could pull in among them," Al said quietly. "No one would pay any attention. We check there regularly."

"You mean where we sometimes catch a few winks?" his partner asked slowly. "Yeah. Guess that is as good a place as any."

"You be the judge," I snapped. "It's your lives. I don't have one to worry about. Get moving."

"That's gospel," Al said coldly. "You got the drop on us now, but the minute you get away, the first officer that sees you will shoot you down like the mad dog you are."

"I'll swim that river when I come to it," I said. "You concentrate on driving."

I finally felt the cruiser bump over a curb, then the cabs of big brewery trucks were visible, with the trailers towering above my line of vision. We eased through the canyon of trucks for a brief minute, the cruiser stopped.

"Here we are," Al said with a stiff voice.

I rose cautiously from the floorboards, holding the riot gun lightly as the blanket dropped from my shoulders. Nothing but trucks all around us.

"Out," I snapped. "Out and climb into one of those trailers. Drop your pistols first!"

They took their pistols gingerly from their holsters, laid them on the seat. Then got slowly out of the cruiser.

"Don't raise your hands," I warned. "Al, come around and join your partner. That's it. Now don't move as much as a muscle while I get out on the other side of this car. Keep your heads turned."

"All right. Now walk over to that trailer," I said after I got clear of the cruiser. "Keep your backs to me! Good."

I vaulted up into an open trailer, covered them with the shotgun again, had them climb up with me. Then I took their handcuffs and fastened them back to back.

"You will be able to get down without getting hurt if you take it easy," I cautioned. "I'm going to leave the keys on the cruiser seat. Wait five minutes and then start getting loose."

I jumped from the trailer, put the riot gun and the keys on the cruiser seat, unhooked a flashlight from the dash, tried it to make sure it burned.

"I'm still around," I called softly to them in the trailer. "Be sure and wait awhile. Hate to kill you after you've been so reasonable."

I dodged lightly between the trucks, the setting sun throwing huge shadows. I found what I was looking for, went down on my knees. I broke a fingernail before it opened. I eased down, pulled the cover closed; I went down, down into the cool dark until my feet couldn't find another stirrup. I took the flashlight from my coat pocket, played the beam on the gurgling slime in the bottom of the sewer, dropped into the slimy water and felt the coolness run into my shoes.

CHAPTER TWENTY-THREE

I WALKED SLOWLY EAST IN THE SEWER, counting my steps. I wanted to keep track of my distance because sometime I had to come out and I wanted to know approximately where that would be. I put distance between the place I entered and myself, found a branch sewer that went left toward the Ohio River. I splashed down it, gave up trying to dodge the miniature waterfalls that burst over me every time someone flushed a toilet.

Fourteen hundred steps and two branch sewers later, I found a dry place to sit. I sat, turned the light off, put it in my pocket, stared absently into the utter blackness, my mind a total blank. I tried to make my mind work, tired to think.

Circles. All I got was circles. I thought of each in turn.

Sheila Thomson. Dead. Big John, Tim and Jackson, out of the city. Mule still around. Lefty dead. Who killed him? The why I knew. It would make the police double-kill crazy. It did. Barby, how did she figure? And the Frenchman, the one at Beverly Hills, Stella's husband. Stella—was she more than a nymph? The knifer—what was his name—Blinky? The gorilla from Chicago? The two punks out at 69 Orchard Road? The old harridan—Mrs. Leeds? Some of them couldn't be the boss—or could they be? How did I know? Did I ever meet the boss? Might be Mike at the saloon. Him with his Cadillac. What about Hogarth? Cops went crooked before. My mind kept trying to tell me something, but everytime I reached for it, it slipped away.

I had to find the key now. There was no more time.

I dropped my head in my hands. Someone among those had to be the boss—or had to be able to contact the boss when they wanted to. The boss couldn't depend on a one-way means of communication. Had to have someone to tip him—or her—when something was happening. Probably by phone, but that would be good enough. If I could get to that person, I'd make them contact the boss on my terms. There would be no way for them to get out of it—not once I got my hands on them. If I could just get on the trail!

The miniature waterfalls made a soothing sound. The cool dark made me realize how little sleep I'd had for the past few days. My eyelids were heavy. Weariness was creeping through me. It didn't get dark until nine this time of the year. I couldn't come out of the sewer before ... before it got dark. I wriggled around, got settled. I let thoughts, impressions, memories flit idly across my mind.

I woke up in the darkness with the eerie feeling that I was buried alive. Cold fingers played along my spine until the tinkling waterfalls made my mind slip into gear. I sat up slowly, stretching the kinks from my cramped muscles. I got the flashlight from my pocket, flashed it on my watch. Ten forty-five. Time to be moving.

But I sat still, thinking of Big John and the time I had put the drug into the drinks.... getting away one jump ahead of the police after tangling with the gang at Mule's place ... of Hogarth almost catching me with my pants down at the apartment.

My heart skipped a beat, stumbled over itself. I came involuntarily to my feet, breath whistling between my teeth, as the whole pattern came tumbling and crashing together in my mind, forming a chain of linked steel.

My mind, my body congealed, went cold and abstract. The deadly game of hide and seek was over. I had the link of the chain that was one—maybe two—links away from the boss's neck. From this moment every move must be calculated and sure, every step planned and executed. One misstep and the pat of the gravedigger's shovel would be at the bottom of the fall—my fall.

I oriented myself in the cool, odorous sewer, started walking. I counted each step, watched each turn. I knew where I was going. I wanted to get as close to the place as possible underground. When I came into the streets, every step I made would be with the expectation of a whining slug from a police gun. I counted the steps north, the steps west, feeling my way under the hostile city, going by dead reckoning to one place.

I stopped, backtracked in my mind over the maze of tunnels I had traveled. I should be close. I watched for the next shaft going straight up. I found it, put the flashlight in my pocket, jumped lightly and grabbed the iron stirrup. Going up slowly, I stopped with my head touching the iron cover. I waited. One minute. Two...

The ripping sound of tires passed overhead. I noted the direction the car was traveling by the sound, that the wheels hadn't passed directly over the steel cover. I waited, hanging on the stirrups, until five cars had ripped sibilantly by. Not one wheel had touched the cover. All had been going in the same direction.

I put one hand against the cover, pushed. It stuck. I poured strength through the arm, my teeth locked together. The cover gave slightly and I instantly relaxed, afraid of flipping the cover too high. I raised it gently until an inch crack showed. Light played on the raised rim, grew brighter. I held the cover steady. The light jumped into the crack, then faded as the stutter from the exhaust snicked by.

The rim of the cover stayed dark brown. I waited until it paled to a lighter shade, started counting. The car passed at the count of twenty-two. I waited for the next. It passed over at the count of twenty-five, followed closely by two more. If I jumped from the sewer when the rim was dark, I had twenty-two seconds to clear the street and find cover before I was lighted by car lamps. The rim of the cover suddenly flared bright, faded as the sound of tires went by, going the other direction.

I was in the middle of a two-way street.

The thought of going back down and finding another outlet was worth considering. But it would probably be in the middle of some street, too, maybe one with more cars.

I shifted my position, raised the whole cover an inch from the street. A dozen cars went by before the rim remained dark.

I raised the cover six inches, hunched my eyes above the level of the street. One car was six blocks away, three cars were four blocks away in the other direction, waiting a stop-light. I couldn't see a person on the street in any direction.

I flipped the cover over, vaulted from the hole, shoved the cover in place and sprinted for the shadows. I ducked between two houses, looked up and down the street. Satisfied that I had not been seen, I looked the street over carefully.

I was on Park Avenue, in the five hundred block. Pretty good dead reckoning. Not too far to go. I moved from shadow to entrance way to shadow, always when no cars were close. Several times I waited while people hurried by. It was twenty-four after twelve when the twin towers showed up in the skyline. I slipped onto the lawn.

I watched and waited for ten minutes before I stole quietly up to the big front doors and twisted the knob around to the left twice before the door eased open. I slipped in, closed the door softly behind me. Looked up to the first landing on the stairs. A dim light was reflected back from the landing. I went up the steps, hugging the wall, down the hall to where the door was standing ajar. I went through the door in a rush, closed it behind me, leaned against it.

Barby jumped up from the bed, the negligee floating free as she came to her feet.

"Toddy!" she cried. "What on earth has happened to you? You're wet—that blood on your shirt! Where have you been? You look a—a mess." She came toward me, a strained smile on her lips, her high breasts quivering under the nylon. "Oh, Toddy, Darling. I've been so worried. The police have orders to shoot you on sight. They've ordered all persons from the streets. How in the world did you get here?" She placed both hands on my shoulders, her eyes looking searchingly into mine.

I brought my right hand up and wrapped my fingers around her lovely face. I shoved with a sudden savage whip of my shoulder, she went stumbling and sprawling backwards, hit on her bottom and slammed against a full-length mirror built into the wall. I bounded across the room, grabbed a handful of her negligee and shortie night-gown, hauled her to her feet, pressed her back to the mirror. Slapped her face back and forth with the flat of my hand.

"You conniving slut!" I rasped, cold anger eating at my vitals. "You worthless, murdering bitch. I want answers—and I want them fast!" I slapped her again, watched blood trickle from a busted lip.

"Toddy," she moaned in appeal and submission. She slumped, a dead weight in my hands, her eyes looking pleadingly into mine. Two big tears slipped out and coursed crookedly down her cheeks.

"Toddy!" she screamed, her eyes fastened on something behind me.

I was already whirling, ducking low, my hands coming to rest lightly on the floor, bent in the form of a sprinter at the starting line.

The sandy-haired bum in the middle of the floor suddenly found the gun in his hand pointing at Barby. His lips pulled back in an anxious snarl and he started to chop the gun down. He never made it.

I took him full in the gut with a looping right fist that bent him double, exploded spit and mucous from his gaping mouth. I closed both hands around his skinny belly, lifted him high and threw him into the big youth standing just in the door, holding a blackjack helplessly in his one hand. The crash shook the mirrored walls of the room.

I stalked over, gently kicked one, then the other, on the point of the jaw. I heard their teeth splintering. I stooped, took them by the hair and pulled them into the middle of the room. Went back and closed the door. Turned to Barby with a pulse of fury beating in my eyes.

Barby had the backs of both hands pressed to her mouth, sobs shaking her body crouched against the mirror. I walked over and looked down at her. I felt something go out of me. Something settled down in my stomach that felt sad, empty and lonely.

"Thanks for the warning," I said bitterly. "But it was unnecessary." I tipped my head in the direction of the wall length mirrors. "I expected a welcome committee. I watched them come in the door. I'm through making any mistakes, Barby. You understand?"

I took her by an arm and lifted her to her feet, led her over to an armchair. I went over and sat on the edge of the bed.

"You're not the boss," I began quietly. "You could never be that hard and unemotional. But you're close to the boss. Close enough to tell me who it is."

She looked at me mutely, twisting her hands under her full breasts. She took a deep, shuddering breath.

"I'm waiting, Barby," I said gently. "I'm waiting because I think you meant all those things you said and did with me. Because you warned me twice when you should have been eager to see me dead.

"That's why I'm not breaking you in little pieces. That's why I want you to tell me who the boss is—tell me what you know. I don't want to tear it out of you, but I will if I have to."

"I'm—I'm not sure I know," she said in a trembling whisper. "I've only talked with the boss on the phone, and the voice has been disguised."

"Who do you think it is?" I asked gently, ignoring the pulse hammering in my head.

"Frenchy," she said wearily. "The waiter at Beverly Hills—the one that waited on us when I wanted that order of sauerkraut and wieners. I had been given orders to get acquainted with you, bring you out there."

"Who gave you the orders? Why bring me out there?"

"I got the orders the usual way—by phone," she said listlessly. "I said that it wasn't part of the deal. I wasn't supposed to use my body and face to lure men—I was supposed to introduce gamblers among the wealthy. I'm the only 'in' they have with the better society," she explained simply.

Go on.

"The boss told me there were other ways I could be made to use my body." Barby shivered. "I've been around too long not to know what the boss meant."

"Why did Frenchy want to meet me?"

"He's awfully sharp on sizing people up," she said bitterly. "I ought to know. He's the one that knew that I was penniless when my parents were killed. He's the one that could read me well enough to know that I would be good for the gambling ring."

"And what was the verdict on me?" I asked dryly.

Barby smiled faintly through swollen lips.

"He said that it would be impossible, even when I tried to argue him out of it." She looked down at her twisting hands. "After—after that first night I didn't want them jumping you."

I didn't ask why to that. It was plain on her face. I felt a gladness trickle through my iced veins. But now wasn't the time to go soft.

"Besides introducing the gamblers to society, what other duties did—do you have?"

"I collected money from certain of the places and banked it." Her eyes were pleading for understanding. "I passed whatever word that the gamblers gave me to the boss. The boss always gave orders direct to his men. If they had any questions later, they called me and I called the boss to get an answer."

"So all the gambling rats know you?"

"No," she said flatly. "I was only a phone number to most of them. A lot of us are known only by phone numbers."

"You have all of those phone numbers—or most of them?"

"Yes," she said simply.

"I haven't got much time," I said sharply. "I'm going to ask some questions—I want a simple yes' or 'no' for answers."

"I'll try."

"You can contact the boss by phone?"

"Yes."

"Can Mule contact the boss by phone?"

"No. He only has my number."

"Do you know where he is right now?"

"Yes, but—"

"No 'buts'!" I snapped. "Does the boss know where he is?"

'Yes. I told the boss. I had to."

"Could the boss phone him right now?"

"Yes." Barby was looking at me with alarm. "What are you planning to do?" she asked anxiously.

"I'm trying to form a plan to get my hands on the boss," I rasped. "But I've still got a few questions: do you know Stella? The Frenchman's wife?"

"So you've met her, too," Barby said wryly. "How did you like the hundred dollar fleshpot? Don't tell me you weren't having any," she asked scornfully, but a hurt look shadowed her green eyes—or was it jealousy?

"I've met her. Have you ever thought of her being the boss?"

"Her? That damn whiskey guzzling hundred-dollar whore?" Barby asked incredulously. "She doesn't have sense enough to get out of bed after a man has had his fill of her."

"Why are you so positive she's nothing but a hundred-dollar whore?" I rasped. If she only got a hundred dollars, she was selling it below market price, but I wasn't going to tell Barby that.

"I ought to know!" Barby said scornfully. "I've paid her the money enough times."

"You?"

"Of course. Part of my—of my job. One of the gamblers spots a big spender wanting a girl, he calls me. I call Stella and she goes to the place and makes his acquaintance. Then she shows him a good time until his money is gone. She knows how to handle them so that they end up in a big game someplace."

"And I guess her husband knows all about this?" I asked sarcastically.

"Of course." She looked at me with wondering pity in her eyes. "You're still a little boy when it comes to sex, Toddy. They teach it in schools now. Don't you know that? About half the married people I know don't care about the other half having an innocent affair once in awhile. Some of them even like for it to happen. Get a kick out of it."

"Maybe I'm old-fashioned," I said stiffly.

"Or maybe being a hypocrite with yourself," Barby said mockingly.

"Did you set Stella on me?" I asked harshly.

"No!" Barby said, half-amused. "I thought I was taking good care of that part. But if the boss had ordered me to do it, I would have."

"I'm not here to discuss my sex life," I said rudely. "Did you sit in on that deal to frame me the other night? Did you have anything to do with the police being after me now?"

"The other night I was there," Barby said in a small voice. "They wanted me to get you in a position where they could—could kill you easy. I wouldn't go along with it. Mule and Lefty didn't want any part of it either. When they started talking about the murder—". She paused, lips trembling. "Toddy, I've never been mixed up that deep with them before! Helping them take a little money away from the rich didn't hurt anyone. Even if I went to my rich friends and told them what I had been doing, they would get a big laugh out of it. It would have been something for them to brag about: playing cards with big time gamblers and not knowing it. A huge joke, even if they were the ones that had the joke played on them. But murder! Toddy, I've been sick inside ever since."

"Yeah? How come you were able to tip me off today?" I snapped.

"The boss called me," she said dully. "Told me to pass the word: that anyone could take a shot at you and earn the praise of the police."

"And you called the gamblers you knew and passed the word?" I asked harshly.

"I had to," she said miserably. "But I went out to a phone booth and put in that call for you."

"You went out to a phone booth?" I asked, a horrible suspicion dawning in my mind.

"All the phones the members have are tapped," Barby said simply. "Most of the members don't know that, but I do. I'm the one that has to pass the information along to Mike when there's a change to be made."

"Then—then the phone at my office has been rigged?" I asked hoarsely. All those people calling in—thinking that it would be safe ... I had to get the boss now.

CHAPTER TWENTY-FOUR

"IN YOUR APARTMENT, TOO," Barby said dully, continuing. "I even know the phone in your apartment is unlisted."

"Mike!" I said with the fury beating at me again. "The one that runs the saloon under my apartment."

"Told you he was a former fighter, didn't he?" Barby said listlessly. "He isn't. He got his face all mashed up fooling with a booby-trapped switchboard during the war."

I suddenly felt naked, trapped. Every move I made, every word I said—the boss knew almost as soon as I said it or made it. Barby saw the sudden mute question in my eyes.

"Yes," she said simply. "I knew you long before I met you. I passed the information along to the boss from my end, who else was giving him information.... well, you guess."

"Even my getting that very apartment wasn't left to chance, I suppose?"

"You mentioned to the clerk at the hotel that you first stayed with that you wanted to get an apartment, if you could. Even told him what you were looking for. He passed the information along.... if you get a chance, look under the sills on those big windows. Everything you ever said in that room was recorded."

"Why? Was I that obvious when I first came here?"

"You stood out like a sore thumb," Barby said amusedly. "Asking leading questions, trying to butter up to gamblers, throwing money around. Some of the boys wanted to take you, but the boss was a little cautious. He thought that maybe you were somebody from Washington. He couldn't find anything out about your background, not until the police got your fingerprints. Then he wanted you on his side, thought that you would make a real good member in his organization.

"Why didn't you, Toddy? Why?" she asked it hopelessly. "You could have everything you wanted, everything—" She saw the look of cold scorn in my eyes.

"You got everything you wanted?" I asked harshly. "Mixed up in a murder, betraying your friends, not calling your life your own? Not even having privacy on your own phone? Not knowing what minute the boss might get tired of your being around? It's been wonderful, hasn't it?"

"I didn't mean it that way," she whispered. "I meant that you and I—that you wouldn't be fighting for your life now. That I wouldn't have to live with the thought of you being—being riddled and torn by bullets." She finished on a shuddering breath, hands twisting at the negligee.

"I'm not that way—yet," I said coldly. "With your help, I won't be. You know you're going to help?" I asked softly, the fury beating in my eyes again. "If you want to or not?"

"How?" she asked, her eyes suddenly big and round with fear.

"You're going to call the boss," I said simply. "You're going to tell the boss what I tell you to."

"I have to make the call, is that it?" she asked timidly.

"Yes, with or without persuasion. That's your only choice, you make it." I got up from the bed.

"If—if I do, and what you have planned fails, you know they'll find me floating in the river?" she asked in a trembling whisper.

"If you don't call, you might not live to get to the river," I ground out, sick with the effort of saying it.

"Toddy! Please, I'm going to make the call. I'm tired—tired of all of it. Until you came along, it didn't really matter, but now—damn you, why didn't you stay away? I was happy, anyway. Now I'm sick, and tired, and all mixed up." She got up resolutely from the chair, stuck her trembling chin out. "Let's get the boss. How do we start?" She couldn't quite make the brave act come across. Her hands kept trembling.

"After you make this call, you have only one out left. Are you ready to face that, too?"

"What do you mean?" Fear was in her eyes.

"You've got to turn yourself over to the police. If I get the boss or not, because that will be your only chance of—staying alive. If I get the boss, some of the gang might think it wiser to remove you before the police get to you. If I don't get the boss—well, you've answered that. Go to the police and turn State's Evidence. At least you'll be safe."

"Maybe the boss is one of the police," she said worriedly. "That's been the great fear of the members all the time: never knowing who the boss was—and scared to even ask a question to find out."

"The boss couldn't be all the police," I said harshly. "To turn State's Evidence is still your only chance."

"There is enough of the old Barbara Medina left," she said quietly. She spread her trembling fingers, looked at them critically, much as a man will do when he's getting ready to shovel coal. She took a deep breath, arching her front-pieces, watched the trembling in her fingers subside. "What do you want me to do?"

"Call Mule," I said slowly. "Listen carefully, because you have to get it right the first time."

She listened, her eyes watching mine, doubt and hope mingling as I strung the trap out. When I finished, her bruised lips tried to smile hopefully. I watched the smile die and panic take its place.

"But you'll be there!" It burst from her. "With Mule and the boss—if you can get through the police going there. They will be waiting for you to walk in the room."

"Not walk into the room," I said savagely. "I'm not going to walk into that room; I'm going to take lock and hinges and the door into the room with me. But if I can time it right, I'll hide in the hall until the boss starts into Mule's room; I might even surprise Mule and have him open the door for me before the boss gets there. I'll face that problem when I get there. Now you get on the phone!"

Barby looked at me with a troubled frown. Her eyes pleaded with me to understand. She walked over to me, looked earnestly into my eyes, wrinkled her nose at the sewer stink on me.

"Toddy—," she said resolutely, "—please be patient with me. When I start talking on that phone, you're going to hear language you never heard from me before, Guttersnipe language. But it's not the real me talking, it's the person the boss wanted talking.

"The first lesson I learned when I got in with this crowd was that education wasn't going to be appreciated, that when I was dealing with the boss or any members of the group I was to use street urchin's language—to save my big words for the times I spent with my society friends. The boss said that the people I would be dealing with couldn't understand anything but dirty words, so I had better learn some and get used to using them.

"Please, you won't be disgusted with me?"

"Do whatever you have to," I said quietly. "I'll not judge you, ever. If we live to see any tomorrows, I'll remember you were on my side when the chips were down, and if you still want me hanging around, I'll be glad to."

"Thanks," she said, tears forming on her eyelids. She went on tiptoe and brushed my lips with her bruised ones, walked over and picked the receiver up, dialed.

"Mule? This is phone Amex 1-2930. What the hell you been doing, you stupid sonofabitch, letting your phone ring so long?" Her voice had a mean, nasty edge to it. "Don't answer me, you thick-headed jerk, that woman-killing sonofabitch might be listening at your door this minute. Want to get your filthy hide mangled? Now you listen to me and keep your hole closed, else you end up on a marble slab.

"You're to keep mum, not even answer your phone, no matter how long it rings and no talking. That guy's wandering around in your place right now, listening at doors to hear your voice so he can get your fat ass. So lock your door and keep it locked, understand? When someone beats it five times, let them in quick. They got a bundle for you and a way to get you out of town until the big guy is bumped or the police nail him.

"You got that straight, you stupid pimp? Keep your gun ready and your mouth closed so we can get you out of this mess. If it was up to me, I'd let the guy get you, you stupid bastard, but the boss wants it this way." She slammed the receiver on the cradle, wiped a shaking hand across her forehead.

"Your plan had better work," she said jerkily. "Your Barby's a dead duck if it doesn't."

"You'll have company," I said softly. "Me and as many as I can take with me."

She got up, walked over to the night-table, poured two shots of brandy into glasses, brought me one. She touched her glass to mine, downed the warm liquid.

"I needed that," she said. "Now for the boss."

One of the guys sprawled in the middle of the floor groaned. Barby jumped and dropped her glass. "Can't have that. Might tip the boss if he does it while you're talking." I walked over, kicked the one under the ear that had started moving his head around. He went back to sleep.

Barby sat weakly on the edge of the bed, took a deep breath and picked the receiver up, looked mutely at me and crossed two trembling fingers. She took a deep, deep breath, held it, let it out slowly, dialed.

"Hello. This is Amex 1-2930," she said excitedly. "The fat's in the fire, sure as hell! Listen, that dumb bastard Mule is cracking. He said that he knows your name and that he's running to the cops! He said you had better get him out of town and get him out in a hurry or he's going to shoot his trap off and get protection from the lousy cops." She stopped talking. I heard that metallic sound blatting on the phone.

"How the hell should I know how he got your name?" Barby whined. "No, I didn't ask the bastard. I don't want to know who you are. You'd better do something or well all be in jail!

"Mule said that he wanted you to bring him a couple of thousand dollars so he could blow town for awhile—get away. Said you had to bring it yourself, he wouldn't trust any other sonofabitch, 'cause they might have orders to kill him. Said that you couldn't afford to do it yourself. Said that you send anyone else he's going to blast them the minute they walk in the door and call the police." Barby listened to that metallic grating, looked at me with excitement in her eyes.

"Yes," she said. "The bastard said for you to knock cops don't know where he's holed up. Not yet, least on the door five times and he'll let you in. No, the he said that he seen none. No, he said no phone calls—someone might be listening. He's in a helluva state, from the way the stupid bastard babbled on the phone. You do what you want. No, I can't go. He wouldn't trust me—said to keep away. I tell you he's scared, probably got crap in his pants. You'd better take care of him in a hurry. He said he was only going to give you a half hour, and that's been ten minutes ago." Barby listened, turned white.

"No!" she said frantically. "You got me wrong! I liked the guy, but I'm not going to jail for no jerk. I'd kill him myself if he walked in the door. God, you think I'm stupid?" she listened for a minute, put the receiver sloppily back on the cradle, checked it to make sure it was resting firmly. Slowly she sank forward and rested her head on the outstretched arm still gripping the phone, her long tawny hair hiding her face.

"It's up to you now," she said dully, her voice muffled by her hanging hair.

"Barby—" I walked over to her, lifted her gently to her feet, looked into her eyes. They were wide with fear. "It's over now. One way or the other, you're free." She started trembling violently. I shook her gently. "Don't break now! You still have a date with the police."

"No!" she moaned, twisting, fighting in hysteria against my hands gripping her shoulders. "No! Please! I can't—the boss will kill me! Don't you understand? The boss will kill me! It won't work—it can't work. The boss is suspicious—he asked me if I had taken sides with you—if I had double-crossed him! Please—"

"What's Mule's address?" I bit out sharply. "His address? Barby!" I shook her until her head whipped.

"The second floor—apartment two," she gasped. "It's 518 East Tenth Street."

"I'll apologize later, Darling," I said gently.

I hit her cleanly on the point of the jaw, caught her sagging body and laid her gently on the bed.

"No mistakes, Toddy," I said to myself aloud, bleakly taking the hypo from my coat pocket, the small capules from the envelope. "No mistakes—no room for mistakes."

I eased the hypo needle into the thick vein on her right arm, pressed the plunger slowly, the way I saw Doc do with me, the way I saw it done when I had helped hold hostile patients, back at the Naval Hospital. I extracted the needle, held my thumb over the puncture. I slapped and shook her head gently with my other hand. She opened her eyes slowly, the pupils dilated, the eye blank.

"Barby, I'm Roscoe Todd. Do you know me?"

"I—know—you." The words were spoken slowly, slurred.

Five minutes later I got up from my knees, looked down into her open, blank eyes. A gladness was singing in my veins, the world had a new meaning. When the chips were down, Barby had leveled with me.

I picked up the phone, dialed the operator, told her to send the police. I couldn't leave her with the two punks lying on the floor. They had heard her warn me, even while I had been roughing her up. When they woke up, the thwarted lust for me would turn on her. She would need another ten or twenty minutes before the effects of the drug wore off. I wanted the police by her when it did.

I swept the room with my glance, went to the bathroom, washed hastily, rummaged in Barby's pocketbook, got her car keys. I went into the hall, down the steps, opened the front door, then closed it softly and quickly.

A police cruiser was gliding up to the curb.

Barby's car was useless. Couldn't get it now—I looked at my wristwatch: five of two. Had less than a half-hour to get to Mule. Once the boss walked in on Mule, I had about one minute before the boss tumbled to the trap. Never make it on time by foot—I turned and raced back through the hall, into the kitchen. Slipped the catch on the back door, went into the back yard, over the back fence into an alley. Down the alley at full run, my shoes were slapping the pavement. The framework of the L&N Railroad bridge swept the star-studded sky less than a block away.

One open street to cross between the bridge and my pumping legs. Police would be as thick as fleas on a dog's back around here in minutes—I slid to a stop by the street edge, looked both ways, then drove across the street and into the shadows of the alley.

The banshee wail of the sirens opened up in the quiet night. The nearness of three of them startled me. One of them was coming directly down the street I had just crossed. I glanced over my bobbing shoulder, saw the shaft of a spotlight whipping around on the street behind me. I put on a desperate burst of speed, dove headlong for the safety of the bridge abutment. The cruiser stopped at the alley mouth, played the spotlight carefully over the garbage cans and trash, hung for an eternal minute on the bridge abutment.

The spotlight went abruptly out. I heard the cruiser move further down the street. The bridge was starting to tremble under the weight of the scheduled freight train that I had silently cussed many a night.

I went up the steel lattice work, swung around a girder, on up until the cross ties were even with my eyes. I paused, looked down toward Barby's house. Headlights, spotlights, sirens were making a bedlam of the night.

The bridge was shaking from the approaching train. I scrambled up beside the roadbed, swung around a steel pillar, hung on, my feet dangling over sixty feet of black nothing. I waited until the engine had rolled and rocked by, eased back around the pillar, held on with one hand, waited for a coal gondola. As I grabbed the iron stirrup with one hand, my body slammed into the steel side of the coal car. I got my other hand on the iron stirrup and scrambled up and over the side, dropped to the sharply angled floor, rolled down into the dump box, sneezing coal dust.

I huddled there and listened to the sirens converging on Barby's house, watched the streetlights sliding by. I got up and peeped over the side, waited until I saw Tenth Street come creeping into sight. I quit the car on a dead run, slammed into an alley beyond Tenth, pelted down the alley. Three blocks to go—thanks my lucky stars that all the police in Newport were heading for Barby's place.

The town, except for the wailing sirens, was quiet with the quietness of a graveyard. I made two blocks with flying feet. Now I had to go out in the streets, look for house numbers. A coldness was growing in the pit of my stomach, every nerve ached from the strain. I slipped down the street, hugging the walls of buildings, silently cursing the deep shadows and cold white light of the crazy moon, turned the corner on Tenth Street, searched it with my eyes aching from the intensity of my concentration.

No police cruisers parked. The street was silent and dead in the white light of the hunting moon. I checked the number of the building on the corner, drew a deep breath. Two houses to go.... I came in the street entrance, my feet hardly touching the pavement as I ran silently on tiptoe, thankful that the moon was throwing deep shadows on my side of the street. I went in the side door, up the steps, still as silent as the wind, except my heart was pounding and the bleak savage fury was pulsing in my eyes again. I hugged the wall of the hall, afraid a board might squeak if I walked in the middle. The first door had a lopsided '1' painted in white on it. Had to cross the hall to the door on my left.... I stepped softly, once, twice—the letter '2' showed dimly. A crack of light glowed from under the sill.

CHAPTER TWENTY-FIVE

WAS MULE WAITING THERE FOR THE KNOCK? Was the murdering bastard waiting with drawn gun, his little pig eyes moving nervously in his insensitive, animal face? I stood there, listening for what seemed ages to my heart pound, not hearing anything but my heart and breath fluttering by my lips. Was Mule alone? Or was the boss there with him? If I knocked on that door and the boss was there.... pistol bullets would come ripping through the door....

"You can't live forever!" I said savagely to myself. "Kirk's killer is waiting for you in there!"

I raised my hand, knocked lightly, standing to the side of the door frame, then crouched, ready for anything.

"Come in, Mr. Todd!" The voice was cold, hard, deadly. "Or would you rather fall in when I shoot through the door?"

I twisted the doorknob, slammed the door open, jumped sideways into the room, went forward on hands and knees, started a spring for the small figure seated in a straight-back kitchen chair. Froze.

"You!" It burst from me, congealed the blood in my veins.

"Get up! Slow!" the dry hard voice directed. "I don't want to shoot you kneeling on the floor."

I watched the gun in the small gloved hand, turned my eyes to Mule, sitting slumped against the wall. He had a big third eye in the middle of his forehead. No, the eye was small, powder burns made it big. The gun must have been shoved against the skin before the trigger was pulled. The smell of raw whiskey tickled my nose, coming from the shattered bottle lying in a puddle on the floor by the table where my host sat. I got slowly to my feet.

"Close the door!"

I backed over and shut the door, holding it an inch from the sill. I might need to get out the door in a hurry—didn't want to take time to twist the knob. Walked slowly over to the woman sitting in the chair, watching the gun in the small gloved hand.

"Catch!" she said suddenly, throwing the gun at me.

Instinctively, I snatched it from the air, held it on her. I wanted to pull the trigger, to start blasting, but deep down in my mind I knew that the gun wasn't loaded—couldn't be loaded.

"Your stake money is still in the bank," she said quietly. "All you have to do is sign for it."

"After I ruin most of your gang—you still want me on your team?" I asked hoarsely.

"Matter of business," she said dryly. "You're better than the part you wrecked. Mule—" She waved a gloved hand in his direction, "—killed Lefty and Sheila. Also your Kirk, whoever he was. I can let Barby live—yes, I heard the police sirens just before I got here. So I knew you got to your dear Barby, but knew that I would have to kill Mule because it would be only minutes until you got here. As I started to say, I can let Barby live, if you marry me."

"Marry you!" It tore from my constricted throat, set devils to hammering at my brain.

"It would be pleasant. I have millions of dollars, but can't spend it. My public life says that I live on a pension, but if I marry a man that has money—that would be different."

"How did you do it?" I asked. "How did you build such a gambling empire?"

"It started when I was in the hospital," she said with complete frankness. "I met a wounded soldier there that knew this town. I backed him with five thousand dollars—after he got the gang organized with me being in the background, I killed him. The rest was easy."

"As easy as killing Kirk, Sheila—the other big shot gamblers! Why did you kill Sheila—why not me?"

"Mule was supposed to kill both of you," she said softly. "He bungled—no, I made a mistake: I didn't know about your terrible strength. I couldn't believe that what you did to Big John was intentional. I thought you had a bit of luck. Then Sheila had been holding out on her bank deposits. When she got orders to pay up she ran to you. She knew better than to ask Big John for it. Holding out money on me is a capital crime in my organization. So now the slate is clean. Mule is dead for your Kirk, for Sheila, for Lefty. I have no opposition in this town. The other big time gamblers are—gone."

"You're going to get the police off my back, I guess?" I asked sarcastically.

"The witnesses are dead," she said simply. "We slip out of here, I furnish you airtight alibis—I can do that, easy—and the police are gone. Easy as that."

"Barby's turned State's Evidence by now," I said, the fury beating at my eyes again. "That's not so easy to fix!"

"The bitch!" she snapped. "But a call from you would fix her. A woman can always change her mind—a little difficult, but Jerkins could handle it. I've played along with you—I've leaned over backwards to get you on my team, I've answered your questions," she said harshly. "You going to be dead in five seconds or am I going to be a married woman?"

"One more question?" I asked softly, madness jumping in my stomach, the urge to mash and tear quivering at my finger tips. "You kill me here—you're finished!"

"I'm your secretary," she said mockingly. "I came here because you called me. I didn't know that you and Mule were going to have a shoot-out. Very convenient my getting a job with you—wasn't it? I'd been waiting for you to hire someone for your office—so when you called, I got there first. Oh, I've had your phones tapped for a long time. I might even carry on with your business after you're gone—give me something to do if you won't marry me."

"Then you arranged that murder trap for me in Ft. Thomas?" I asked, awed at the complete monster this woman had been turned into. "Why—why all this murder, this leeching for money? Because you have a steel leg? Because men wouldn't have you?"

"What else has Sarah Loren, ex-Marine and ex-woman, got to live for?" She patted her metal leg. "Expect me to live for this? For the pity of women and the scorn of men?" Her lips twisted into a sneer. "The good women with their good pity, the good men with their good scorn! I make them wallow in their goodness—their dollar high goodness!" she spat it.

She looked like something out of a horror movie, sitting at the table, the broken whiskey bottle at her feet, Mule sitting grotesquely against the wall with the hole in his forehead. Her face was twisted, the eyes two flaming holes under the eyebrows. The single overhead light bulb made the wrinkles in her face even harsher.

"You should never have called me at my apartment," I said, my voice dropping to the zero level of my control. "That is an unlisted phone and Barby was the only one that had the number. I had to step on her to get to you, you unholy bitch!"

"I'm offering you your life—a better one than you ever had!" she blazed, her eyes afire. "I can't stay here any longer—I dropped the whiskey bottle to cover the shot when I killed Mule—but someone might have heard. Do we join hands or do you die?"

"Stick it!" I snapped in sudden snarling rage.

"Pull the trigger, lover-boy!" she snarled, her voice ugly and sick with emotion. "I need your prints after I put this gun in Mule's hand!" Her hands unfolded in her lap, the blue shine of an army forty-five colt sliding out from under her light summer coat. "I gave you a chance. I didn't want it this way! Pull the trigger, you damn fool!"

"You dumb murdering bitch!" I flipped the gun into her snarling face. Let the fury in me boil over.

The .45 was sliding free from her coat, racing the pistol whistling for her face, swinging in a wicked blue shining arch to line up on my guts.

Her eyes widened suddenly in terror, the pistol crashed into her face, the .45 roared before it completed its arch, the slug flipping my coat under the armpit. The roar echoed and re-echoed in the room as I grabbed her by the mangled crew-cut and lifted her dangling like a rag doll from the chair, started my balled fist whistling toward her contorted face.

"Drop her!" a hoarse voice bellowed. "Drop her, you mule-headed Irishman!"

I let loose of the mangled crew-cut, let her drop onto the chair, watched her bounce off, fall sprawled in the whiskey on the floor.

I turned around, all my senses suddenly dull and unfocused.

Detective Sergeant Hogarth stood just in the door, one hand gripping his service pistol hugging his left shoulder, three uniformed police, with .03 rifles, flanking him.

"Good," he said between clamped white lips. "If you hadn't dropped her, we would have had to blow you apart."

"But I didn't—"

"Didn't do any killing?" he rasped laboriously. "So we just heard. But you caused me to take the slug meant for you in my shoulder—couldn't quite beat her to the shot."

"You shot her?" I asked blankly.

"Yeah. Got it off a second too late—but I think I'll live."

One of the uniformed police crossed over to her, put his hand under the summer coat, pulled it back bloody.

"Dead," he said quietly.

"Save the taxpayers some money," Hogarth grunted, letting himself be led to a chair by a poliecman. "You ready to go peaceful?"

"Yeah," I said wearily, slumping into the chair Sarah Loren had warmed. "Yeah, my job's done. How did you get here so quick?"

"Been here all the time," he said with an effort. "Knew you would try to get to Mule. Thought you would get to him if you got by us. Been in the apartment across the hall since dark. Didn't know you were in the building until you knocked on the door. Started to take you then, but she—," he inclined his head weakly toward the sprawled body, "—threatened to shoot you through the door, so I waited."

"Didn't you hear the shot when she killed Mule?" I asked with wearied annoyance.

"Naw. Heard a whiskey bottle bust," he said, hugging his shoulder tighter. "Saw her knock on the door with the whiskey bottle, go in. Thought nothing of it. Man wants a dame to kill the time—we could attend to that later. Drops the bottle when he hustles her to the bed.... hell, I can't know everything. When in hell is that police ambulance going to get here?" He looked at me balefully. "Take this Irishman to jail. Not that I think he'll stay there long, but we've got to hold him. Few things to answer for."

"You think up a good story to tell the papers while you're in the hospital," I said sincerely. "I'll back it. That's the way lieutenants are made."

"Bribes, huh?" he said nastily, but a grin was on the edge of his lips.

"No," I said shortly. "A reward for a good cop. One who can add two and two twice and come up with eight. Besides, you got a girl down at headquarters that has turned State's Evidence. On your side now. She'll need a break."

"First I heard of it," he said with interest. "Been converting as well as roughing them up, huh? Well, she plays ball, we'll play ball, if she hasn't killed anyone?"

"No," I said softly. "She hasn't even hurt anyone but herself. How long will it be before we get out of jail?"

"Four or five years," he said, clamping his teeth on sudden pain from the shoulder, brushed the sweat from his forehead with his sleeve, smiled weakly. "But with a lieutenant pulling for you—maybe four or five days, who knows?"

"Thanks," I said.

"Yeah. The same to you. Just wished you had stopped this slug before it got to me. In slight payment for the ruckus you caused. Now get the hell out of here and let me hurt in peace until the ambulance comes."

Two of the police stepped to my side. I turned and walked out with them, looked back over my shoulder at Hogarth, smiled. He grinned weakly back. I went down the steps and into the moonlit night, with Kirk's face smiling happily back in my memories. I stopped suddenly.

"Hey, Sergeant!" I shouted to the building.

"Yes?" I heard his faint answer.

"Just for the book—Kirk was my twin brother! He got adopted from the orphanage—I didn't. That's why we had different names."

I turned to the officers, looked at their curious faces, shrugged and crawled into the cruiser.

The two officers booked me on a 'hold' warrant, escorted me to the bullpen. One pointed to the wash-rooms.

"Don't dirty the bed." He wrinkled his nose at the sewer smell of my clothes. "Clean up first."

I did. Afterwards the hard cot under the barred window welcomed me with the warmth and softness of a feather bed. I drifted off into black nothingness, Barby's pert face wrinkling its nose at me....

"What a poor liar you are!" Barby smiled blithely, hanging on my arm as we walked down the courthouse steps. "The District Attorney swallowed the hook, but he's bouncing the sinker around in his open hand."

"Uh huh." I paused on the last step, looked over the wide lawn at the drowsing town. "But Sergeant Hogarth has a good chance at the lieutenants list—say, did you see that little plastic disc Hogarth was twisting around in his fingers?"

"You mean that odd-looking good luck charm or whatever it was?" Barby grinned at me. "Silly men! Thinking a piece of celluloid can bring good luck!"

"Silly women!" I snorted. "Good luck charm—yeah, if you call assorted murder and mayhem good luck! I asked him where he got it and the dumb gluck said he found it sticking on the mouthpiece of the phone in Mule's apartment—wondered what it was doing there!"

"You don't mean—," Barby looked at me with wide eyes, "—but of course! That's what made her voice sound so—so creepy!"

"Uh huh. But enough of the idle chatter—you got work to do. A lot of things to settle at the office—that lawyer of mine is attaching Loren's estate. I get ten percent of the gambling claims settled."

"Me—work?" Barby looked at me, then wrinkled her forehead. "But I don't have a job—not any more. You took care of that." She looked up into my eyes. "Thanks," she said simply.

"Not too fast with those thanks," I said with mirth under my eyelids. "I got you another one. You still have to earn your keep— so, as of this morning, you are Mr. Roscoe Todd's private—and I mean 'private' secretary."

"Oh." Barby twisted her mouth to one side, made her big eyes innocent. "Mr. Todd, sir—," she lisped in school-girl mimic, "— how much dress above the knee do you require? My teacher said that that depended on the boss-man."

"This is a brand new boss-man." I took Barby by the elbow and headed for the office. "Never was a woman's boss-man before. This boss-man will have to find out about that part of the job—never a better time to find out about secretaries than now."

THE END